THE CROWLINGS

by the same author

Journey Through Llandor
The Road to Irriyan
The Shadow of Mordican

Moonwind
Warriors of Taan
The Power of Stars
Children of the Dust

THE
CROWLINGS

LOUISE LAWRENCE

Collins
An imprint of HarperCollins*Publishers*

First published in Great Britain by Collins 1999
1 3 5 7 9 10 8 6 4 2

Collins is an imprint of HarperCollins*Publishers* Ltd,
77-85 Fulham Palace Road, Hammersmith, London W6 8JB

ISBN 0 00 185726-6

A CIP record for this title is available
from the British Library

Set in Tepolo Book 12.5pt
Printed and bound in Great Britain by
Caledonian International Book Manufacturing Ltd,
Glasgow G4

SMALL FRY

The boy sat cross-legged beneath the awning, a woven blanket draped round his shoulders. The cooking fires died, and the Wolf-clan slept in their tents, but he stayed awake. Night-long, without moving, he listened to the night-hawks hooting in the forest and watched the pale mist drifting above the lake.

When the stars faded, the land slowly became visible again and the sun rose behind him, casting long tree-shadows across the sundried grass. Furry goupas scampered from their burrows and stuffed their pouches with its seeds. He could see the mountains rising beyond the lake, fir woods dark on their flanks, and the cleft peak of Skadhu pink and shining with freshly fallen snow.

He wondered what he would see tomorrow after he ran, and fell, and slept, and woke again. He wondered what creature would appear for him from which he would take his name. A thousand possibilities flittered through his mind. He murmured them softly in his own tongue. He murmured them in the language of the star-people who had conquered his planet. Ooni the woodjay ... bakkau the stone-lizard ... luppa the wolf.

Finally his clan people awoke. Women rekindled

their cook-fires. Men took their spears and went hunting. Children splashed and screamed in the shallows of the lake. Un-named, unheeded, and no longer one of them, the boy watched and waited.

This was the third day he would sit alone beneath the awning. He was very tired, very hungry, but he had to resist his desire to sleep or eat. He had to resist the offerings his parents placed at his feet, the gourd of goat's milk and platter of fish. If he would pass from boyhood to manhood he could not accept sustenance from them.

Their eyes looked questioningly down on him, his mother's as pale as amethyst, his father's deep purple as the juice of belberries that grew on Skadhu's heights. Their voices murmured, "Child, will you eat?"

"Child, will you drink?"

"Child, will you return and share our tent?"

It was the third time of asking and for the third time the boy shook his head and watched them walk away. Now he was released from them and no longer their child. He was no one to anyone, unperceivable and non-existent, until tomorrow when he found his name and was received back into the clan as a grown man.

Baxter crawled from the Luppa's tent, zipped his jeans and strode towards the forest to relieve himself. He would pass right by the place where the boy was sitting, a tall gangly man with pale skin, strange blue eyes, and hair the colour of the stars from which he came. He had lived with the Wolf-clan for most of the summer, an alien from another world, learning their language and studying their ways.

The boy had learnt much about aliens since Baxter had come to stay. There were millions of them, Baxter had said, settled in the towns and cities beyond the dry plains. They had taken over the lands of the Hump-ox and the lands of the Bison, the lands of the Fisher-folk and the lands of the Long-river clan. Eventually they would claim the lands of the Wolf-clan, too, Baxter reckoned. And many times their flying-machines had passed above the forests surveying for oil and minerals and taking aerial photographs. He urged the Wolf-clan to move out. Far to the south there were territories set aside for the native people where they would be left to live in peace, he said.

But the council of warriors refused to hear him.

They would fight if they had to, Luppa declared.

Baxter winked at the boy on his way to the forest. "How're you doing, Small Fry?"

The boy flushed with annoyance. It was forbidden to heed him, forbidden to speak to him, and Small Fry was his childhood name. He was not the son of Brown Trout any more, living with the reek of smoked fish, and nor did he want to be. He wanted to be more than his father. He wanted to be a warrior, or a hunter, or a tracker ... snow bear or mountain cat or luppa, leader of the Wolf-clan when the present Luppa died. Even more, he wanted to be karrakeel, one of the winged guardians of his world, and unite the clans as a single people.

There was no word for the karrakeel in Baxter's language. They were fabulous and legendary, unseen for many lifetimes. But the stories said that when the need arose they would waken from their centuries of sleep and leave their tomb beneath Skadhu. He would run that way, the boy decided. He would run towards Skadhu, the Shadow Mountain. He would fall, and sleep, and wake to see the karrakeel circling above him on their shining wings. He would hear their voices and know he was the chosen one. He would rally the scattered clans and drive the aliens away. He would drive Baxter away, too, if ever he called him Small Fry again.

The star-man grinned as if he guessed the boy's thoughts. "Have a nice day," he said.

It was a long, hot day. The sun beat on the awning and the boy's head swam. A few sips of tepid water from a goatskin flask was all he was allowed. He longed for the night's coolness, the fire-dance and the final run. Brown Trout, his father, had not made it past the shores of the lake, but the boy would run further. He would leave the forests and the hunting territories behind and reach Skadhu's heights before he fell.

He gazed at the cleft peak standing stark against the sky. Nearer, on the lake-shore, men and children stacked driftwood at the water's edge. Among the tents women stirred their cooking pots, prepared for supper and the boy's naming feast. When he returned there would be bread and meat and honeyed fruits spread on the grass. He would don clay beads, a leather skirt and a fur-lined mantle, the garb of a man.

On its own beneath the trees, on the edge of the campsite, was the tent that would house him. A group of girls, close to himself in age, painted symbols on its leather sides in bold, bright colours. He could hear them laughing and, now and then, they glanced in his direction. They knew, tomorrow, one of them would become his wife.

Who he chose depended on the creature whose name he shared. No self-respecting girl would wed a Slime-worm or a Stink-rat, except Cloud perhaps. Morose and scowling, with a twisted foot and running to fat, Cloud would be lucky to find a husband at all. Certainly Small Fry would not ask for *her*. He would ask for Shawna, perhaps, named at her birth for the morning star, or Shavanni, named for the ice-flower that bloomed in the forests in the depth of winter. Both were lissom and pretty. But their faces blurred as he considered them and the landscape shifted and spun. He vomited bile on the dust.

The hunters returned in late afternoon with the carcass of a deer, and Brown Trout beached his canoe and hung his string of fish to dry in the next day's sun. Cooking smells drifted on the breeze, churned up the emptiness of Small Fry's stomach as the clan families gathered to eat, Baxter sharing the Luppa's food. It was a time for being together, but not for Small Fry. His only companions were the glow-worms and flittermice and one of the sledge-dogs who paused to lick his face.

Twilight deepened and the nightbirds stirred. The mountains dissolved into darkness and another alien flying-machine winked among the stars. Then, when the first moon rose above Skadhu, and the women and children retired to their tents, Brown Trout lit the beach-fire.

Flames flickered brightly. A wild drum beat and, young and old, the clan's men came to summon Small Fry to their midst. They were robed and masked, apart from Baxter who was dressed as he always was in a checked shirt and jeans. Human forms with heads of birds and animals and reptiles, fish and insects, gestured him to rise. Weakened from his long fast and three days of sitting cross-legged on the ground, his limbs failed to support him. He fell helplessly, and hot shame burned his face as a strong hand gripped his arm and hauled him to his feet.

He barely remembered entering the circle of firelight. The drum-sounds beat through his head as he downed the shaman's draught, winced against its bitter after-taste. But his strength was renewed and the chill liquid sloshed in the hollow of his stomach as he began to dance.

At first he felt heavy and cumbersome, at odds with the rhythm of the drums, the stamping of feet and clapping of hands and men's voices chanting. But it grew easier after a while. His body felt lighter, and the music possessed him, taking over his mind.

Then he was not himself but everything ... earth and water, fire and sky. He was the drumbeat and the reed pipes wailing, the masked faces surrounding him, scale and feather and carapace, antenna and fur. He was the lake and the forest and the unseen mountains, the pale sheen of starlight on Baxter's hair.

"Go for it, Small Fry!"

"Don't call me that!" howled the boy.

His voice went unheard. His pride and anger blazed like the fire and was consumed. He was the bright flare of sparks against the sky, the burned branches crumbling to ash. And still he danced ... until the music and chanting stopped.

Heaving for breath, he paused in a moment of stillness and silence. The second moon had risen above the mountains, silvering the lake water lapping nearby and bathing the forest with eerie light. Then the hissing began ... the crowing, the barking, the snarling and growling and slavering. Eyes glittering from monstrous faces filled him with terror. They were no longer men, but beasts who would tear him apart.

Small Fry had barely enough strength left to run, yet he did run, leaping the embers of the fire and heading along the lake-shore with great loping strides. He thought they pursued him, but when he turned towards the forest he saw they were ahead of him, their black shadows lurking among the moonlit trees.

His terror grew, and he veered towards the marshes at the far end of the lake. His legs sank in bog. Rotting branches and reed beds barred his way. Step after step he had to haul himself on. Stems of sedge cut his hands. His lungs strained, and his muscles ached, and he knew why his father had fallen.

There was no shame in being Brown Trout or Water Snake. No shame, when his feet found firmer ground, to fall and sleep and wake to become Yellow Snail crawling through the mosses or Green Frog sitting on a willow stump. But Small Fry had dreamt of himself as a hunter or warrior and made himself go on, forcing a path through tangled thickets bearded with lichen, losing all sense of direction.

He thought he would fall in the mire-woods, but the trees finally gave way to an open hillside topped with weathered pines. He knew where he was then, heading in the direction he had intended in spite of himself. This was the place where the fish-hawks nested and if he must fall he would do it there.

Weary and shaking, Small Fry leant against a tree trunk, gazing back the way he had come and far beyond. He could see where the forest gave way to the plain, an ocean of grass on the distant horizon. Maybe, if he climbed higher, he would glimpse the lights of the alien cities and wake to see an ice-bear, or a fire-eagle, or even the karrakeel.

He turned to ponder it. Ridge beyond ridge, the slopes of the mountains rose towards the sky. The cleft peak of Skadhu swayed as he swayed and its snows glittered like the stars. He knew he would never reach the highest regions, the frozen scree and barren crags and scouring glaciers, but he could cross the peat-moors and climb the ravine beside the waterfall.

The first moon had set behind him and the second was hidden by towering cliffs when he entered the ravine. It was loud with the sound and movement of a torrent, dark water dashing against rocks. Deeper in and the sound increased, the dull deafening fall of Skadhu's cataract that allowed no other awareness. There was just it and himself, veils of noise and shimmering motion and the pains of his body telling him to stop. He wept with the need to sleep, but the wet spray soaked him, and the cold was intense. He knew he would likely die if he lay down now.

He began to climb upwards beside the waterfall. He climbed in darkness, his fingers and toes searching for handholds and footholds in the face of the cliff. Wider ledges offered him places to rest, but always the cold drove him on. His feet grew numb and his fingers froze, but slowly the skyline came nearer, and finally he hauled the heavy weight of his own body over the rim and onto the water-slick rocks at the top.

After that he crawled. He crawled through ferns and tussocks of grass and stunted rushes. He crawled across stones and dust. The thunder of the waterfall faded behind him and the night grew silent. The only sounds were the sounds he made and the moan of the wind around Skadhu's heights.

A dry gully sheltered him and he lay exhausted. Too weak to stand or even raise his head, he never saw the lights of the alien cities – Jasper's Creek, New London, Ohio Town. His last strength gone and no longer caring what his name would be, Small Fry slept. He did not dream that when he awoke his life would be changed for ever.

He woke reluctantly, disturbed by a sound, lay in a half-drowse and listened. He could feel the sun warm on his shoulders, the aches of his body, and his own mind urging him to sleep again. He did not remember where he was or how he came to be there, but when he opened his eyes he could see the ground on which he was lying, a grey rubble of stones among grey dust. Leaves of a thorn-briar fluttered, scarlet with the season, and there were tiny scratching noises behind him.

He turned his head and the stench hit him. Not far away, on a level with his face, was the carcass of a marrou, a mountain sheep. It was little more than a tangle of bones and fleece, a broken rib-cage hanging with scraps of flesh. But the skull was intact. A white woolly countenance with great curved horns gazed blankly through the empty sockets where its eyes had been.

He stared at it uncomprehendingly, and from deep within its skull something stared back at him, the twinkle of a living eye in the cavernous darkness. It was beady and malevolent and it was not alone. The dead head was crammed with them, alive with their movements and sounds, the almost imperceptible chittering and chirruping, the clicking of beaks and the tiny scratching of claws.

Kiku, he thought in disgust. Crowlings in Baxter's language. They were carrion-eaters, scavengers, birds as small as flittermice, their sharp-toothed beaks tearing away at every morsel of flesh. It was them he could smell, the reek of their droppings stronger than the reek of death.

One crawled through the sheep's nostril. Its small bald head was smeared with blood, its black feathers sticky with gore. Too bloated to fly, it disgorged from its stuffed crop several pellets of semi-digested pickings, then perched on the curved horn to preen itself. Stubby wings fluttered. Scarlet feet with tiny claws raked and scratched as Small Fry watched it.

It was named for its call, its softly murmured piping ... kiku, kiku ... and nothing in its name to tell its nature. Baxter's name was better, a small crow as murderous and loathsome as the crows of his world but even more so. A kiku would eat dung or vomit, flies or maggots, anything that was alive or dead. It would peck out the eyes of dying goats or sickly children, and a large flock could strip a hump-ox of its meat within an hour. Stink-rats were sweet compared to crowlings. Bloody droppings splattered the sheep's white face and Small Fry turned away his head.

It was then that he remembered why he was there, lying face down in a gully high on the mountains. It was then he recognised the significance. In a moment of overwhelming horror he realised he had found his adult name. He was Crowling, Kiku, the death bird. He beat his clenched fists on the earth.

"No!" he screamed. "I won't be that! I won't be!"

Leaping to his feet, howling and shouting and maddened with rage, he kicked at the carcass and watched it explode. Crowlings poured out of every cranny, scurried from its skull and its rib cage and the hollows of its bones. Heads bloodied and beaks shiny with marrow, they moved in a black twittering tide, tiny distended bodies and scarlet legs scuttling through the dust. He kicked and stamped and killed, trying to destroy the hateful name he could not wish to share, but there were too many of them. Beneath the tangled branches of the thorn-briar and among stones he knew they survived, and he was Crowling still.

He stopped, defeated, chewed a strip of pemmican from the pouch at his belt and gazed round. He heard a fire-eagle mewling above the mountains and raised his eyes to the blue overhead sky, hoping to see it. He could lie, he thought. He could be Fire Eagle not Crowling. No one would know, except himself. He waited to see it sail into view and saw instead a grey shape squatting on a rocky outcrop at the rim of the gully. The unblinking yellow eyes of a fully-grown bakkau gazed down on him, and its tail thrashed menacingly.

Small Fry's heart hammered in sudden fear. He reached for his knife, then changed his mind. The stone-lizard was twice his size. Its great jaws could snap him in two with a single bite. His only option was to run. The black tongue flickered and the bakkau made its dash, but it was slow, sluggish, its reptilian blood as yet unwarmed by the sun. Its full belly sagged between squat legs and he reached the forest before it.

Green shade surrounded him where the bakkau would not follow. It needed the sunlight of Skadhu's open slopes and the marrou to feed upon, not the haunts of deer and woodjays, the familiar hunting territory of the Wolf-clan. Fearless now, Crowling slowed his pace, smiled to himself and thrilled at the memory. No one at their naming had ever returned as Bakkau, but *he* could be Bakkau and it was not exactly a lie.

Making up his mind, he headed for the waterfall and by noon he was back in the ravine. He honed a length of sapling, speared a fish and grilled it over a small fire. Then with his hunger sated, his bruises and grazes cleansed and soothed by the icy water, he continued homewards.

"I am Bakkau!" he called to the sky and the moorland.

"I am Bakkau!" he told the fish-hawks on the pine-topped hill.

"I am Bakkau!" he shouted to the Wolf-clan.

The wind carried his voice across the mire-woods, across the arrow-shaped lake lying blue and still beneath the afternoon sky. At the far end, between the water and the forest, he saw the smoke of the clan's cooking-fires. Or maybe it was not? It was black and thick and billowing and there were flames where no flames should be. The tents burned and the Wolf-clan was being attacked.

"No!" screamed the boy to the spirits of the dead

who guarded them: Bakkaus of the past, and Wolves, and Wood Dogs, and Fire Eagles. "No!" he cried to the soul of the ice-bear on Skadhu's heights and the lost karrakeel. "Don't let it be! Don't let it be! Please, don't let it be!"

Nothing answered him except the fish-hawks wheeling and crying above the lake and a tiny bird-like sound among the fallen twigs at his feet – kiku, kiku. Small and black, a single crowling fed on the fish-rich dung beneath the pine trees, reminding him of who he really was and what kind of man he would be. No warrior, no hunter, no defender of his people, but a scratcher in the dirt for other people's leavings, an eater of poop.

Sickened and terrified, Small Fry drew his knife and began to run. Plans formed in his head, and he remembered the tales Brown Trout had told him to while away the long winter evenings in the log-house. The Wolf-clan had been attacked before, although not in Small Fry's lifetime. But when Brown Trout was a child, warriors from the Bison-clan had slain the Luppa and dragged away his wife and daughters. The present Luppa had made peace with them several years ago at the great gathering, but the hatred remained and the blood-debt had yet to be paid.

Whoever it was now who ransacked their camp and burned their tents – Bison, or Hump-ox, or warriors of the Long-river people – they would live to regret it, Small Fry thought fiercely. He would circle through the woods and come at them from behind, untether and stampede their horses and release their prisoners. And then he would fight. He would fight like the Bakkau he was meant to be and spare no one.

Small Fry waited, dry-mouthed and motionless among the shadows, the knife clutched in his hand. He could hear no noise. The raiders were sleeping, he thought, stuffed with nuts and dried fish and pemmican, the supplies the Wolf-clan had gathered throughout the summer. Unless they had taken their spoils and were already gone?

He moved cautiously, creeping around the moth-willow coppice. Smoke from the burning tents drifted on shafts of sunlight as he approached the open grassland and the shores of the lake. Someone was standing among the smouldering debris, a solitary man, tall and lean and indistinguishable, his head bowed as if in mourning. Small Fry held his breath and his fingers tightened on the knife as he crept forward. But a dry twig cracked beneath his feet and the man turned round.

Baxter's blue eyes were reddened from the smoke, his face, hands and clothes blackened by soot. "You're back then?" he said.

"Yes," said Small Fry.

Baxter nodded grimly. "Lucky you didn't get here half an hour earlier. If you had you'd have been dead by now."

Small Fry stared at the charred heaps of leather that had once been tents. Blackened bodies lay among burned crocks and cooking pots and smoking bed-rolls. He saw fragments of cloth, an ivory comb, a string of clay beads gripped in the bones of a hand.

He saw Brown Trout's strings of fish and the remains of his own naming feast trampled into the grass.

"They can't have killed everyone!" he cried.

"All but the few who escaped," muttered Baxter. "That club-footed girl and a couple of dozen kids."

"They killed the women, too?"

"No," said Baxter. "They took them with them, all who were old enough to bear children and young enough to work."

"But they didn't kill you!" Small Fry said accusingly.

"I wasn't here," said Baxter. "I was at the ruins in the forest, digging for artefacts. The girl and the kids came there to find me and when I returned it was too late. The murdering devils were already leaving."

Small Fry bit his lip. There was a rage of pain inside him. He wanted to weep. But he was a man now, the only man left, and all he could do was hate. "Who was it?" he asked.

Baxter shrugged. "Bison?" he said. "Bison by their head-dresses. Or maybe Hump-ox masquerading as Bison? That's happened before. They take someone's territory knowing we, the star-people, want it, then do a deal with us. Money, concessions, land-grants – we pay them to do our dirty work. And who's worst? Us or them?"

He spat in the ash at his feet and his face twisted. "The Luppa should have listened!" he said. "It was bound to come. We always get what we want one way or another. We don't do it directly any more as we did on our own world, but we're doing it indirectly and the result's the same."

"I don't understand," said Small Fry.

"You will," said Baxter.

Small Fry watched as the starman turned towards the forest and cupped his hands. "It's safe to come out now!" he hollered.

Several minutes later they appeared from behind the moth-willow brake, a group of dark-haired children with tearstained faces, boys and girls dressed alike in white loincloths tied at the waist. A few wore beads round their necks or coloured sweat-bands round their heads. And Cloud came waddling behind them, small ones clinging to her skirt, a sleeping infant in a sling across her breast.

Competent and stolid, she stood beside the single tent that remained intact: Small Fry's marriage tent. She spoke no words but her deep purple eyes, undampened by tears, issued a challenge. She was the only girl left of marriageable age and she had proved her worth. She had saved the children. And if he would have a future, become a man in any way other than name and rebuild the clan, then he must do it through her and take her to wife.

Small Fry shuddered. Cloud would accept anyone, even a man who bore the name of Crowling. But he would never admit who he was and nor would he ever have her as his mate. His scowl outclassed hers. He would sell her, he thought, at the next great gathering, trade her and a couple of younger girls for a girl of another clan who was more desirable. Guessing perhaps, she shrugged indifferently and looked to Baxter for the approval Small Fry refused to give.

"You did well, girl," the starman told her.

"Will we leave here?" Cloud asked him.

"I reckon," said Baxter.

"I'll make ready," she said.

All the more Small Fry hated her. "I'm the clan chief now!" he said. "It's for me to say whether or not we leave!"

"There's nothing to stay for," said Baxter.

"I'll make ready," Cloud repeated.

She laid the baby on the grass and gathered the children round her, sent the girls into the forest to search for nuts and berries, and had the boys cut moth-willow branches to weave a drag-sledge. Baxter went to help and, increasingly annoyed, Small Fry turned his back. In the absence of anyone older, and as self-proclaimed head of the clan, he should be deferred to, but Cloud and Baxter took over, both ignoring him.

He left them to it. Shifting camp was women's work anyway and he had other, more pressing, duties. The spirits of the dead would haunt this place for ever unless someone sent them to their rest. He must perform the rites of passage to the afterworld, release them from their bonds to the living and sing their souls farewell. He squatted on his heels amid the carnage and raised his arms, his voice keening across the lake calling their spirits one by one and bidding them go.

Nearby the children gathered the remains of his

naming-feast from the grass, and Cloud dismantled his marriage tent and strapped it on the drag-sledge. Boys whistled for the sledge-dogs, but none of them answered. Only the milk-goats came skittering home from the forest, fearing the howl of the luppa as the twilight deepened. Small Fry sang on, arms folded now across his chest and his head bowed, aware of none of them until Baxter placed a hand upon his shoulder.

"Time to go, Small Fry."

"I'm not ready yet."

"Everyone else is ready."

"I'll follow later," said Small Fry.

"You'll lead," Baxter said sternly. "You're the clan chief now and those kids are your responsibility. They need to get away from here."

Angrily, Small Fry rose to his feet. Baxter understood nothing of their ways. "Children are women's responsibility!" he said scathingly. "Tell Cloud to take them to the log-house where we spend the winter. She knows the way."

"Tell her yourself!" Baxter retorted. "And what's the point in going to the log-house? The raiders could return and slaughter you while you sleep. We're going south to the Reservations. You'll be safe there, all of you."

Small Fry's anger grew. No one but the Luppa, together with warriors and hunters gathered round the council-fire, had a right to make that kind of decision. And Small Fry was the clan chief now, not Baxter.

"I say what happens and where we go!" he said fiercely. "These are the lands of the Wolf-clan and we won't abandon them, not for you or anyone!"

The starman shook his head. "There *is* no Wolf-clan now, Small Fry! You're all that's left of it and you've got no choice! If you want to go on surviving you've got to go south. That's where we're heading anyway, me and the girl and the kids. You do as you like, but we're not waiting!"

He strode away, hoisted the handles of the drag-sledge and slipped the traces over his shoulders, a man doing the work of a dog. Cloud followed, carrying the baby, and the children followed her. Older girls lugged toddlers. Younger ones carried skins full of drinking water and bundles of food wrapped in charred pieces of cloth. Boys drove the goats, and others bore broken spears, bows and arrows and skinning knives, a few salvaged belongings stripped from the dead. Southwards, they headed into the shadows of the forest, and alone among the ghosts of the Wolf-clan Small Fry watched them. None of them looked back at him, not even Cloud.

No soul could be banished into the darkness, so Small Fry was forced to wait until dawn to complete his task. The loneliness was intense. Chilled and hungry, with no tent to shelter him or mantle to cover him, he kept watch over the dead. He thought of Cloud and Baxter and the children, wondered where they were, how far they had gone and if he should follow them. But he had to stay for the spirit of Brown Trout and all the other men he had not yet named, woodsmen and bow-makers and carvers of canoes, the apprentice weather-dancer and the retired storyteller. Cross-legged on the ground among their charred bodies, he sat and remembered. He reminded himself that he was a man now and must not weep, but the child within recalled his mother, cried for the loss of her and finally slept.

"Kiku ... kiku."

He woke at first light when his namesake called him, a black scrap of life in the grass at his feet, the reek of it stronger than the lingering smell of smoke and the miasma of death. Bead-bright eyes regarded him warily before it scuttled away to join its companions. And everywhere he looked, he saw them, thousands upon thousands of crowlings. The ground was black with them. Red feet scratched among the ashes. Toothed bills tore and pecked. They feasted on the burned flesh of his kin, fled as he screamed and stamped, and returned to feast again.

Small Fry howled and kicked and ran and flapped his arms. He needed the pungent oil of bearsbane to keep them away, but the flowers were long over and the shaman's brews were gone. And he alone could not defend the bodies of the Wolf-clan. His feet were bloodied and stuck with feathers and still the birds returned, scavenging multitudes flying in from the forests and the mountains, whirling and fluttering like black leaves in the sunlight. Wings brushed against his face as he beat against them.

"Kiku ... kiku."

Their small cries surrounded him. One landed in his hair, pecked at his scalp, and others followed, vicious and biting. He screamed and ran, clawing at the tiny moving bodies, hurling them away until finally he was free of them. Blood slimed his hands and trickled down his face but he did not stop. Southwards along the forest trail Small Fry continued to run, sobbing and hysterical, fearing the main flock would follow.

After a while his panic subsided and he began to feel safe from the crowlings' attack. He bathed in a river creek beside the ford, washed his hair and his loincloth clean of droppings, then crossed to the far bank. There he saw footprints in the mud, traces of a bivouac beneath the trees, and tracks of the drag-sledge leading away along a wide path through the forest. The memory returned of Cloud and Baxter leaving him behind, the anger, too, at being ignored and abandoned. It was bitter anger, greater than his longing to stay within the boundaries of the territory where he had been born and raised, or his need to exorcise the ghosts of the dead.

Cloud had cheated him, he thought. She was his now to do as he liked with, along with all she possessed, and she had no right to go with Baxter. She and the children were all that was left of the Wolf-clan and he was their chief. Cloud must do as he said even if his name *was* Crowling. He would follow her, he decided, pursue her wherever she went. And when he caught up with her he would bring her back and the children with her.

He followed their tracks and, although the river marked the boundary of the Wolf-clan's land, the path was familiar. Every few years, at the gathering place on the edge of the great plain, the various clans would meet for trade and council, and Small Fry with Brown Trout had travelled that way before. The woods thinned by nightfall, but he travelled on until the two moons rose, slept in a bed of leaves and cursed when he woke with the mid-morning sun warm on his face.

Cloud and the children were ahead of him still, but not that far. Shortly after noon he passed their camping place of the previous night, leaves torn by the goats and trampled grasses, and by sundown he stood on the edge of the open plain hoping for a glimpse of them.

The landscape was empty as far as he could see. To the south and east low rolling hills of hummocky grass swept towards a skyline of darkness and stars, and mountains in the west rose indigo blue with shadows. Leaving the forest was a kind of grief, but Cloud and Baxter and the children were only a few hours ahead and if he hurried he might catch up with them by midnight.

He set out in pursuit across the grasslands and his hatred grew, focused on Cloud, her scowl in his memory that forced him to follow. He did not belong out here. It was Bison land, or Hump-ox land, or maybe the star-people's territory. He did not know how to exist in these vast open spaces. The isolation terrified him and, as the darkness deepened, he stumbled over the tussocks of grass and began to lose direction.

Then, somewhere ahead, he heard the eerie cry of an unknown creature. It was answered by others nearby, dog-like howls predatory and menacing. Small Fry understood the ways of wolves in the forest, knew where to hide and how to escape them, but these could be plain-dogs hunting him and he knew nothing of them.

Fearing for his life, he ran towards the mountains. There, at least, he was likely to find a ledge to climb on or running water to hide his trail. Dark miles fled behind him although the animals followed, unseen presences on either side, others circling ahead to cut off his escape. Light from the two moons rising glinted in their eyes.

Then, beyond the shadow-line of the mountains, he saw a tiny flicker of fire. Someone was camped there who might give him shelter, Hump-ox or Bison, no matter who. Desperately he sprinted across the final distance. Grass gave way to dust. Stone walls rose before him, high and ruinous. An abandoned city, similar to the one buried in the forest, sprawled at the mountain's foot. He could no longer see the fire, but it had to be somewhere nearby. Empty doorways beckoned, led into roofless rooms that offered no escape. Paved streets choked with thorn-briars barred his way. His cries for help echoed through the darkness and the dogs howled at his heels.

Then from high on a parapet someone answered, a girl's voice urgent and shrill, calling his name. He saw a flight of stone stairs leading upwards, small boys with burning brands hurrying down with Baxter at their head. Teeth snapped at Crowling's ankle. Others tore at his shin as he fell. The boys came running, yelled and screamed and beat with their sticks. The dogs snarled and released him and Baxter hauled him upright, pushed him towards the stairs.

"Run!" cried the starman.

"Up here!" cried Cloud.

Small Fry could barely walk. She dragged him bodily as Baxter and the boys fought to drive the dog-pack away. Their howls receded and a smell of singed fur filled the night. By then Small Fry was atop the wall. The stairs led down again into a roofless room where children of the Wolf-clan were huddled around the fire, gazing up at him with terrified eyes. He shook off Cloud's steadying hand, limped down the steps and sat on the ground in their midst.

"You want food?" asked Cloud.

"Just see to my leg!" he said curtly.

She frowned at him but she said nothing, poured water from a gourd into a clay pot, added salt from a pouch and set it to heat. Goats, spooked by the dogs, skittered and tugged at their leashes and Baxter returned to cast his burning brand upon the fire. Sparks showered skywards and the children retreated, dragged their tattered blankets and heavy fur mantles to the darker edges of the room.

"We'll have to keep watch," Baxter informed Cloud. "If those coyotes had a whiff of goat they'll likely be back. Lucky we heard you shout," he said to Small Fry. "You'd have been dog-poop by morning if we hadn't. And that wound needs cauterising. Animal bites can turn nasty and I don't want to end up carrying you all the way to the Reservation."

"We're not *going* to the Reservation!" Small Fry said fiercely.

"We can talk about that later," said Baxter.

"There's nothing to talk about!" said Small Fry.

"If you say so," Baxter agreed.

Small Fry watched as the starman took out his pocket knife and sterilised its blade in the flames, then lay on his stomach and gritted his teeth against the pain. Several times Baxter repeated the same torture, and afterwards Cloud took over with the salt water, inflicting more agony. The raw edges left by Baxter's knife seared and stung. Tears gathered in his eyes and he howled his protest.

"You're worse than a baby!" said Cloud.

"You're hurting me deliberately!" Small Fry said angrily.

"Would you prefer the wound to fester?" she asked.

"We'll need something to bind it with," said Baxter.

He folded a spare loincloth to make a compress and Cloud bound it to Small Fry's leg with a leather thong unpicked from his marriage tent. Afterwards, as Baxter arranged the rota of watches, she gave him supper of meat scraps and nut-cake, and had the audacity to question him.

"Did you find your man-name?" she asked.

"Yes," he said tersely.

"Is it Stink Rat?" she inquired.

"No!" he said furiously.

"Goupa?" she guessed.

"Not that either!"

"What then?" she demanded.

"Mind your own business!" he told her.

She handed him a gourd of stale water to drink from and her smirk made an insult of her servitude. "You'll have to tell us one day," she said. "It's who we are."

"Pass me a mantle!" said Small Fry.

"They're for the children," said Cloud.

Later, curled on the bare earth among nervous goats and restless youngsters, with the baby wailing, Cloud hushing it, and Baxter and a couple of boys keeping watch from the wall, Small Fry settled to sleep. Tomorrow, he thought, he would tell Cloud and Baxter what he expected from them. None of them were going to the Native Reservation. They were the Wolf-clan and they were going home.

Again Small Fry slept late. The sun had already risen above the walls of the room, and Cloud had the drag-sledge packed and the children fed before he awoke. Tying the infant in its sling across her breast, she ushered the girls and toddlers up the steps, and the boys followed behind her, driving the goats. She did not even glance in Small Fry's direction. And she had taken the food with her, too. Just a few morsels of venison and a single biscuit lay on a flattened stone nearby. And the fringed leather skirt he would have worn at his naming-feast was dumped on the ground beside him.

Small Fry put it on, the garb of a man hiding his loincloth, and ate his mingy breakfast as Baxter stamped out the embers of their fire. The starman was tall and lean, a head and shoulders taller than Small Fry, his blond hair shining with sunlight. But his blue alien eyes were kind when he turned towards him.

"Need a hand up, Small Fry?"

"I can manage," muttered Small Fry. He struggled to his feet, and his leg throbbed horribly.

"Try this," said Baxter.

He had lashed a cross-piece to a spear, padded it with leather and fashioned a crutch to help Small Fry walk. Then, hoisting the sledge harness onto his shoulders, he dragged it up the stairs, pausing near the top to stare at some carvings on the wall.

"They're the same as your tent paintings," he said. "Bakkau and luppa and that winged reptilian creature you call the karrakeel. Those huge almond-shaped eyes make it look almost intelligent."

"The karrakeel are the guardians of our world," said Small Fry.

"I've heard the stories," said Baxter. "And I've seen them elsewhere, too, carved on other ruins in various parts of the planet. According to carbon-dating they're around ten thousand years old. Yours must have been a great civilisation once, Small Fry."

"No," said Small Fry. "We came from the womb of the mountains just as we are."

"That may be the legend," said Baxter. "But what really happened? Some kind of cataclysm, I suppose. A sudden change of climate or a shift of the planet's axis, maybe? A descent into barbarism. Or maybe you're better off as you are now."

He heaved the sledge up the final steps. Singed fur mantles, insecurely lashed, slipped from beneath the marriage tent and had to be reloaded, and by the time Small Fry stepped onto the parapet Cloud and the children were already heading south. He cupped his hands, bellowed loudly, ordering them to turn back. But the wind, whistling from the east across the plain, carried his voice in the wrong direction and they failed to hear him. Angrily he turned to Baxter.

"Where's she off to? I said last night we weren't going to the Reservation! Go after her and fetch her back!"

Baxter raised an eyebrow. "Let's get something straight," he said. "I don't take orders, not from you or anyone else. And she knows what she's about. Got her head screwed on right, has young Cloud. She'll do what's best for those kids no matter what."

"She'll do as I tell her!" Small Fry said furiously.

"I wouldn't bank on it," Baxter advised him.

Without waiting for Small Fry's response the starman hauled the sledge down the steps. Following, Small Fry hated him, elbowed past him when they reached the bottom and set out after Cloud. He hobbled as fast as he could, his shouts rebounding from the walls of the ruined city, the distance between them slowly decreasing. She glanced back once, but she did not stop, and the wound on his leg tore open and began to bleed again.

He sat on a stone by a ruined wall where Baxter caught up with him and helped him adjust the bandaging. They walked on together through the wind and dust, although neither of them spoke. Small Fry was still fuming and Baxter, apparently unconcerned, whistled a tune from his own world and gazed at the landscape round him.

The ruins petered out, gave way to scree, low crumbling cliffs and dried-out gullies. And the grass in the wind rippled like water all the way to the sky.

"This could be Oregon," Baxter finally remarked.

Small Fry said nothing.

"Not that I remember it much," Baxter went on. "I was only seven when we left. Me and my sister were among the third wave of emigrants to your planet. As a family we were looking for a fresh start. It took us ten years to get here and even before we'd settled in I didn't like the way things were shaping up. Same sort of government. Same sort of social ideals. Same sort of rules and regulations already in place. I headed for the hills at the first opportunity, stayed with various clans and learnt their languages. I'm on your side, Small Fry, if only you knew it."

"If you were, you'd do as I ask!" Small Fry said bitterly.

They were in sight again now, Cloud and the children, a ragged band wandering through the knee-high grass carrying their bundles. Baxter squinted after them into the harsh sunlight, but his pace matched Small Fry's limp and he made no attempt to hurry.

Cloud remained ahead of them. Hour after hour she marched the children onwards, dry grass chafing their legs and the sun burning their faces. Noon became afternoon and still she continued. The children grew tired and fractious, but Cloud allowed no let-up, no pause for food or drink or rest. Then, when the shadows of the mountains spread across the plain and the air grew chill with the coming night, she finally stopped.

The camping place she chose was in the lee of a low cliff that sheltered them from the wind. She had kindled a fire of thorn-briar and was kneeling on the dusty ground dispensing food from the bundles when Small Fry and Baxter finally caught up with her. The goats, already milked, browsed nearby. Crowling waited expectantly. His tongue was parched, his stomach hollow with hunger, but Cloud made no attempt to serve him. She sat suckling the baby on a dug of cloth dipped in milk.

"The children need to sleep," she informed Baxter.

The starman nodded, unpacked the furs from the sledge and spread them beneath the overhang. Girls and toddlers, their tearstained faces grey with dust, crammed their mouths with meat and milk and crawled to their bed. Boys wrapped rags around their hands and hauled more briars for the fire. Small Fry counted twenty-seven in all, excluding himself and Baxter, Cloud and the baby.

Annoyed that his needs were being ignored, he seated himself within the circle of warmth, winced from the pain in his leg, and reached for a package of venison and a loaf of nut-bread. Cloud glanced at him and frowned but again she said nothing. Then, when Baxter came to join them, she laid the infant on the ground and rose to serve him.

"I'm sorry it's not much," she said.

"Where's yours?" Baxter asked her.

"Some of us have to do without so that others can have more," Cloud said pointedly.

Small Fry was incensed. Not only had she snubbed him by serving Baxter food and not him, she was now accusing him of eating her share. He wanted to throw it at her, hurl it in her fat smug face. He watched as Baxter halved his own small portion.

"Here," said the starman. "You can't not eat."

Cloud smiled and accepted. "We might find berries tomorrow," she said.

"How's the water situation?" asked Baxter.

"It might last a week if we're careful," said Cloud.

"A week's not long enough," Baxter informed her.

"Perhaps it will rain?" she said hopefully.

The starman shook his head. "This land's in the rain-shadow of the mountains," he told her. "The further south we go the drier it gets. Those kids won't make it, Cloud."

Cloud nodded determinedly. "We'll do as you said then. Head east in the morning. Find a ranch-house and ask for help."

Small Fry had heard enough. "Where we go isn't up to you!" he said angrily. "It's for me to decide when we leave and what direction we take! And I've already told you we're going north! Returning to our own territory!"

Cloud's dark purple eyes fixed on his face. "We don't have any territory," she said. "It's been taken from us."

"We'll take it back!"

"Without any warriors?" Cloud said scornfully.

"It's ours, I tell you!"

"All that's ours we have with us," Cloud replied.

"We're still the Wolf-clan!"

"No we're not," said Cloud. "The Wolf-clan have been slaughtered. We're whatever you are and you're not a Luppa. If you were, you would have told us by now. You would have bragged about it. So you must be something else, something small and disgusting ... Slime Worm or Crawling Toad or Dung Beetle ... something you don't want to be."

"That's what you think!" raged Small Fry. "But you don't know anything! You're just a stupid girl! And whoever I am you still have to do what I say!"

Cloud rose ponderously to her feet. She was several seasons older than Crowling, taller than him, too, and twice his girth. Her fists clenched and her heavy jowl set and her eyes flashed in the firelight. He flinched when she spoke.

"I may be a girl!" Cloud said harshly. "But I'm also a human being the same as you are! And you don't own me, not out here! You don't own any of us! This is star-people's territory and they're not allowed to own each other! Baxter told me that! You can do as you like, but we're going to the Reservation, me and the children, and you can't stop us!"

She waddled away into the gathering twilight and Baxter cast fresh branches on the fire. "Not one to argue with," he murmured.

"This is your fault!" Small Fry said bitterly.

"Why's that?" asked Baxter.

"Filling her head with alien twaddle!"

"Have you never questioned your own ways?" Baxter inquired.

"Why should I?" Small Fry asked crossly.

Baxter yawned and lay back, arms behind his head, staring up at the stars from which he came. "We made the same mistake back on Earth," he said musingly. "We thought we owned everything and everyone just because we were men. But all slaves rebel in the end and that includes women. Liberation, our women called it, and they could have changed everything. Instead they demanded equality – equal pay, equal opportunities, the right to compete. And the whole sorry mess continued. We had women bosses, women politicians, women soldiers and a world that wasn't worth living on."

"What's that got to do with me?" Crowling demanded.

"Just playing with ideas," said Baxter. "But if you want to hang on to who and what you are, you can't do it alone. You need Cloud, too, her knowledge along with your own. Man and woman, see? One can't survive without the other. And some day we star-people are going to need both of you. We despoiled our own planet, but if we're to save this one from going the same way we'll need you to teach us how to live, you *and* her. You've got to let her be, Small Fry, respect her as she is or none of us will have a future."

Small Fry chewed his lip, heard her footsteps returning, her fringed leather skirt brushing the grasses. The goats nickered in greeting and the baby began to cry. Cloud picked it up, cradled and hushed it and returned it to its wolf-pelt cradle. Small children whimpered in their dreams and she comforted them, too, then busied herself with grinding a porridge of milk and tree-nuts ready for morning.

Hidden by the darkness Small Fry watched her, her girlish bulk blotting out the stars on the far horizon. Baxter was right, he thought. As a man Small Fry could hunt and fish, set a snare, axe down a tree and maybe fashion a canoe, but Cloud could do other things that were equally important. He would never like her, he decided, nor would he ever accept living on a Reservation, but he was willing to acknowledge that wherever they went, wherever their future lay, they would not survive long without her.

In the chill, first light Cloud headed east towards the morning and nothing Small Fry said could dissuade her. She simply refused to hear him. Scowling and obstinate and deaf to all reasoning, she ploughed through the grass with the children following, Baxter and the drag-sledge trailing some way behind. For a while Small Fry hobbled beside her, his arguments rebuffed by her silence, but even with her twisted foot she soon outpaced him. He had no choice but to run, place himself bodily in front of her and bar her way.

"Listen, you!"

Cloud side-stepped, made to move on, but again Small Fry placed himself in front of her. She stopped and stared at him defiantly.

"You've got no right to do this!" he told her. "It's going against everything we are! And I won't let you! Now do as I say and turn those kids around!"

"Try making me," said Cloud.

He raised his crutch and she pushed him, hard, a hand to his chest that sent him sprawling backwards over a tussock of grass. He lay spread-eagled, temporarily winded, and Cloud swept on. Goats and children passed him, boys, girls and toddlers casting curious glances in his direction, understanding nothing except that Cloud had felled him. But Baxter understood, paused with the sledge as he drew level.

"Threaten that girl again and you'll have me to answer to!" the starman said curtly. "So let's have an end to it, shall we?"

He continued on his way without waiting for an answer and, speechless with rage, Small Fry struggled to his feet and stood alone among the grasses. The wind blew in his face and the morning sun lifted above the far horizon. Vast and lonely, in all directions, the hills rolled towards the sky. It was his choice now. He could either follow or return to his homeland. But the forests of his memory were equally lonely, inhabited only by birds and beasts and the ghosts of the Wolf-clan to whom he had once belonged.

He caught up with them at sundown. They were camped for the night in the lee of a hill. Temperatures dipped towards freezing, but the treeless land and the tinder-dry grass prohibited all thoughts of fire. The sledge turned on its side with the marriage tent draped over it provided their only shelter and, when Small Fry approached, the little ones were already sleeping in their bed of spread furs, a few tattered blankets to cover them.

Tired and shivering and unsure of his welcome, he thought to keep himself apart. But without a word and barely a glance, Cloud accepted him back, handed him a water-skin and scraps of bread and meat. Baxter made a space for him among the huddled bodies, saw him wince as he moved.

"That leg giving you trouble?" asked the starman.

"Not particularly," lied Small Fry.

"As well," said Baxter. "We've still got several days of hard walking ahead of us."

For a second night the two moons rose together, silvering the grass and the stubble on Baxter's chin. Awake and watchful, the alien sat guarding the goats as Cloud snored and Small Fry tried to sleep. And at dawn Cloud roused him, doled out the rations, repacked the sledge, and set off eastwards again.

It was pleasant at first. The sun warmed his bones. The children chattered happily. Boys skipped beside him, proud that he allowed them. He was older than them, head of their clan and someone to emulate. They imitated his posture and his limp, restored a sense of who he was and made him feel important again. Then, to please him, they mimicked Cloud, waddling behind her, laughing and giggling. Small Fry grinned at their antics.

"You obviously find it amusing," Baxter remarked.

"Don't you?" asked Small Fry.

"Not really," said the starman. "In my books it's known as mocking the afflicted. And how would you have felt if, yesterday, we'd laughed at you?"

Small Fry shrugged. The ways of the star-people were not his ways, nor would they ever be. And the boys' high spirits ended naturally after a while, their banter and chatter fading into silence as the journey took its toll. Hour after daylight hour they trudged across the plain, Cloud leading the children and himself limping behind, accompanied by Baxter and the drag-sledge.

Days passed. Travelling became harder and they grew wearier, the landscape bleaker and more inhospitable. Thorn-briars replaced the tussock grass and gradually the horizons flattened. Then a great, dry lake-bed spread before them where the ground was baked hard and even thorn-briars failed to grow.

They stood on the edge of it.

"I hadn't reckoned on this," muttered Baxter.

"What?" asked Cloud.

"This area's known as the Flats," said Baxter. "We should have gone further south."

"Would it have made any difference?" asked Cloud.

The starman sighed. "Probably not," he admitted.

Small Fry said nothing. The right to decide where they went and what they did had been taken from him. He left it to Cloud, sat on the baked-mud shore as she set up camp and removed the ragged dressing from his leg. There was no fresh blood on the bandage but the skin around the wound was fiery-red and warm to his touch. He scrubbed it with spittle.

"Problem?" asked Baxter.

Remembering the knife, Small Fry shook his head, left the wound open for the air to heal it, and set out with the rest of the clan the following morning.

Two days out across the lake-bed and their situation worsened. In the flat, featureless terrain there was no escaping from the wind and sun, no alleviation from the cold at night, and the land provided nothing to sustain them. The goats went dry. Their food rations dwindled and their water allowance was down to a few sips a day. Carrion birds circled in the overhead sky and bones of dead bison bleached in the sand.

Their pace slowed. The festering spread on Small Fry's leg. His head throbbed. Thirst and hunger plagued him. Small children wailed incessantly and refused to be pacified, and the older girls had barely enough strength left to carry them. A few of the youngest Baxter hauled on the sledge, but even he grew weary.

And like the starman, they were all equally dirty, skinny as sticks, footsore and sunburnt, their loincloths hanging in tatters. The boys plodded silently, no laughter left in them. Then the water ran out, and the baby began to weaken. They all began to weaken. Famished eyes stared from emaciated faces. And still Cloud drove them onwards, an indomitable force that refused to be beaten. Scolding, chivvying, coaxing, she forced them to walk through yet another day, another long, hot, endless afternoon.

Small Fry sweated and shivered and stumbled. His leg swelled up as far as his knee and burned like fire, seared with pain each time his foot touched the ground, and his weight on the crutch had rubbed his armpit raw. His tongue stuck to the roof of his mouth and his vision was hazy.

He kept his eyes fixed on Cloud, but now and then she seemed to dissolve. Portions of time went missing and when next he became aware of her it was dark. Beside her, Baxter pulled the drag-sledge. Goats and silent children trailed behind, and a strange orangy glow dimmed the stars on the far horizon.

"That could be the lights of Jasper's Creek," said Baxter.

"You mean we're nearly there?" asked Cloud.

"Hardly," said Baxter. "It must be at least thirty miles away. Probably more. But we might find a ranch house that's nearer. This time tomorrow maybe."

"Or in the morning," said Cloud.

"Those kids can't keep going much longer."

"If we stop now we might never get up again," said Cloud.

Small Fry knew what she intended. She intended them to walk all night. But he could not do it, not any more. He felt sick and giddy. Great waves of blackness washed through his mind and his leg jarred as he fell. He lay on the ground moaning with pain. Children gathered round and Baxter put down the sledge, knelt beside him and laid a hand on his forehead. Cloud elbowed her way through.

"Get him on his feet," she said harshly.

"He's burning with fever," said Baxter.

"All the more reason," said Cloud.

"Why not leave him where he is?" suggested Baxter.

"We're not going without him!" Cloud said fiercely.

"Then stay here and I'll go on ahead," said Baxter.

"What good will that do?"

"I'll rustle up a truck to come and fetch you."

"How long will that take?" asked Cloud. "All this night and another day? Maybe another night or more before you return? And in all this land how will you find us?"

"I'll find you," Baxter assured her.

Cloud bent and draped Small Fry's arm round her shoulder.

"You might be too late," she said. "He could be dead by then! We could all be dead! But tonight we're alive, and as long as we're alive we can go on walking, and so can he." She heaved Small Fry to his feet, regardless of his agony. "Move!" she commanded. "Or do I have to drag you?"

She took his weight and he stumbled on, leaning against her. He could smell her sweat, the strong female scent of her body, the sour reek of the baby at her breast and her embroidered leather shift. He could feel her firmness, her softness, her movements, her warmth. She was all there was ... Cloud, as immense as the night itself, a girl of the forest carrying the future in her loins and at times carrying him.

He hated her for what she did, hated her boundless strength and his own feebleness. She seemed not to care how sick he was or how much he hurt, just railed at him each time he faltered and refused to let him stop.

"Walk!" she insisted.

"I can't," he moaned.

"Walk, damn you!"

"I can't! Not any further!"

Finally, she did let him stop. She dumped him on the drag-sledge and covered him with furs, had Baxter pull him and made the toddlers walk. Or maybe she carried them, too? Small Fry did not know. Flat on his back he was unaware of anything except his own agony, the jolting swaying movement of the sledge and the rasp of Baxter's breath. The two moons wheeled and circled in the sky above him and faded with his senses to an infinity of dark.

After that Small Fry remembered in snatches: glimpses of dawn and the sky brightening, Cloud's cry and the excited shouts of children, the sudden jerk of the sledge that almost tossed him out as Baxter started to run. They were in sight of habitation with only a few more miles to travel, but it was almost noon by the time Baxter had heaved the sledge over the rocks and stones of the lake-shore to where the grass began.

Small Fry heard cattle bellowing in the distance, saw fences and a gate and high wheels turning in the wind. Later, a collection of white-walled buildings sheltered by trees. Sunlight flickering through the leaves made a bliss of shade on his face, and alien voices answered Baxter's holler.

Small Fry did not see who they were. He felt sick again. Waves of pain and darkness came and went, and the next thing he knew the sledge had stopped moving, the children had vanished and he was alone. Turning his head to one side, he saw a space of green cropped turf surrounded by bare earth borders and a few faded flowers. And on the other side was a white-washed wall, a brightness reflecting from it that pained his eyes although he lay in shadow. Star-people, a woman and a man, stood and talked in an open doorway.

"I've telephoned the Welfare," said the woman. "Someone should be here within an hour."

"Them kids still need feeding," said the man.

"We're not a charity kitchen, Henry! We can't afford—"

"They're kids, for Christ's sake! They've been walking over two weeks and they're half-starved, all of them! We can give them something at least. And what about this one?"

"What about him?"

"He's sick, Emily."

"He's also filthy dirty! You'll have to put him in the barn with the rest of them. I'm not having him in the house. Why that Mr Baxter had to bring them here I really don't know!"

Their voices faded as another wave of darkness swept through Small Fry's mind. When, once again, he became aware of his surroundings he was lying on his back in a bed of dried grass and someone was sponging his body with icy water. He could hear the rustle of goats, and the whispers of children, a flutter of wings among the roof-rafters and the baby suckling nearby. He could smell milk and hay dust. And strange cooking odours, meaty and oily, wafted through the open doorway.

"Burgers and fries?" asked Baxter.

"There's more to come," the woman said brusquely.

"It's very good of you," said Baxter.

"How's the boy?" asked the man.

"We need more ice," said Cloud.

Later, with a roar of noise, an alien machine arrived. It stopped outside and hot acrid fumes filled the air. Terrified youngsters gagged and whimpered until the noise cut off into sudden silence. Small Fry heard the metallic slam of a door, footsteps on gravel and someone entering the barn. She was a woman by her shape, although she wore jeans the same as Baxter. Her hair was an odd reddish colour, like the ochre paint the warriors used to daub their bodies for the fire-dance. Her voice was clipped and efficient.

"Mr and Mrs Curry?"

"In the house," Baxter informed her.

"Are these the children?"

"Who wants to know?"

"I'm Kate O'Halloran from Jasper's Creek Welfare Department."

"Ah," said Baxter. "In that case, yes. These are the children. And I'm Joel Baxter."

"How many are there altogether?" asked Kate.

"Thirty, including the baby."

"And all of them orphans, I suppose?"

"There are no surviving parents," Baxter confirmed.

"What was it?" Kate asked bitterly. "Another tribal massacre? And what's wrong with the boy?"

"He got bitten by a prairie dog."

"You mean he's hydrophobic?"

"I reckon it's blood-poisoning," said Baxter.

Kate nodded. "We'd best get him to the infirmary," she stated. "I'll drop him off there on my way back to the office. Can you stay on here, Mr Baxter, until I organise transport for the rest of them?"

"I wasn't exactly planning on abandoning them," said Baxter.

"Great," said Kate. "They can stay in the hostel on Fourth Street until we can decide what to do with them. The little ones can be offered for adoption, of course, but God only knows what we'll do with the others."

"Excuse me?" said Baxter.

"In order to adapt to our way of life and become acceptable, they're going to need intensive social training," said Kate.

"What the hell are you talking about?" asked Baxter. "They don't need social training! They've got their own way of life which is a damned sight more acceptable than ours!"

"*And* we want to stay together!" Cloud said fiercely.

Kate paused, and when next she spoke it was to Cloud. "I doubt if it will be possible for you to stay together," she explained gently. "We'll obviously do our best, but with no parents to look after you—"

"We can look after ourselves," said Cloud.

"I'm sorry," said Kate. "The Welfare Department simply won't allow it. Without a responsible adult—"

"What do you class *me* as?" Baxter demanded.

Again Kate paused as her attention shifted. "You have a substantial income, do you, Mr Baxter? Enough to provide food, clothes, and adequate accommodation for thirty children? A wife, perhaps, who will help you raise them? If so, pardon me for misjudging you, but I had you marked down as some kind of hobo in need of welfare assistance yourself."

"Money's not the only criterion for responsible adulthood!" Baxter said angrily. "What about caring and compassion and all the other qualities that categorise us as human?"

"If you truly care, Mr Baxter, you'll do what's best for these children."

"Which is exactly what I intend to do!" Baxter retorted. "I'm planning on taking them to a Reservation. As a displaced tribe—"

"Thirty children with no surviving adults can hardly be classified as a displaced tribe," Kate informed him. "They simply don't qualify for relocation."

"Rubbish!" said Baxter. "If our government annexes their territory, which I bet they do, then these kids are due for compensation the same as any other clan! And I intend to see that they get it!"

"Can we can talk about this later?" asked Kate. "Right now I need to see Mr and Mrs Curry and have them sign the forms for reimbursement. Then there's transport to organise, food and clothes and bedding to find, finance to arrange with the various departments and volunteers to run the hostel. And the older boy needs medical attention. I'll be leaving in approximately five minutes if you'd be kind enough to take him to the car."

Small Fry struggled to sit up. "No!" he said feebly.

"You're not taking him without us!" said Cloud. "We're his clan and we're staying together!"

"If he's not soon treated he could die!" Kate protested.

"Not if we're with him," said Cloud.

"Explain it to them!" Kate said to Baxter.

"There's not much to explain, except to you,"

Baxter replied.

Kate stared at him, then gazed round at the children. "What do you want from me?" she demanded angrily.

"We've already told you," said Cloud. "We want to stay together."

Kate returned at twilight with a yellow bus. One by one, she and Baxter, Mr Curry and the driver carried the frightened children on board. Lastly, Baxter carried Small Fry, laid him on a long back seat and covered him with a blanket. He was vaguely aware of a row going on outside, Cloud loudly insisting the goats travelled with them. "Not on a school bus!" said the driver. And, eventually, Kate and Baxter persuaded her to leave them in Mr Curry's care, temporarily at least until some more suitable transport could be arranged for them. But she would leave nothing else. Shabby fur mantles, the baby's precious wolfskin and Small Fry's marriage tent, were stowed in the boot before Cloud climbed aboard.

The bus drove off towards Jasper's Creek. It was a nightmare journey, twenty miles of noise and stench and sickening motion. Shuddering vibrations wracked Small Fry's body. Heat fumes and gasoline burned his lungs, and ceiling lights shone in his eyes. The baby screamed and the children wailed and vomited. Time after time Kate made the driver stop the engine for them to get out. Only Cloud stayed unaffected. In the roaring, shifting environment, she followed Kate and

Baxter's example, did her best to calm the others and tend the little ones' needs.

She calmed Small Fry, too. In a white sterile room, where a fan fixed to the ceiling blew chill air on his face and torso, she sat beside the metal bed on which he lay. Liquid in a bag above his head dripped through a tube into his arm. His bitten leg was heavily bandaged. He remembered bright lights, aliens in green gowns with masked faces, a needle entering his vein. He did not know where he was or what had happened to him, but it seemed not to matter as long as Cloud was there.

As long as Cloud was there the clan was there also, embodied in her with all the life he had lost. He could smell the forest on her clothes, the night in her hair, the sun and rain on her face and ice-flowers sweet on her breath. She sang as the wind sang in the trees of his homeland and lulled him to sleep.

He dreamed he was a child again dancing through the shallows of the lake. He dreamed of the mountain slopes in summer, blue with flaxen flowers. He dreamed of the warriors hunting. But the wood jay screamed out its warning and he saw again the burned bodies of the Wolf-clan, a horde of crowlings feasting on their flesh. He woke up screaming and Cloud was gone.

Light and whiteness surrounded him. Star-people came running. One, wearing a white gown, held him down by his shoulders. Another stuck a needle in his arm. The next time he awoke the tube and drip bag had been removed. He lay for a long time watching the fan turning in the ceiling, hearing the soft incessant buzz of the lights. The air smelled of nothing and the bare white walls kept out the world and the weather, isolated him from everything that was alive.

Later the star-people returned. A woman checked his pulse and his blood heat, another tried to feed him. He sensed their intentions were kindly, but all he wanted to do was escape from the light and the brightness and the white walls that enclosed him, the stifling scentless air. He tried to tell them, raged and fought and spat when they refused to listen. They called him a savage, left and closed the door, and when he went to open it he found he could not.

Small Fry was trapped and he could not bear it, the terrible unrelieved feeling of being confined. He screamed and howled, beat on the door with his clenched fists until he was exhausted. After that he squatted in the corner and sought solace within himself, covered his head with his arms to shut out the sight. He realised then that his body, too, was scentless, as clean as the room. The star-people had washed away the smell of who he was, destroyed the last connection to himself and the land. Naked and imprisoned, with nothing to sustain him, his only wish then was to die.

When they returned again they found him crouched on the floor, inert and unmoving. They lifted him back into bed but he would not respond. He simply lay there, curled in a foetal position and not wanting to know. Someone pulled up his eyelids and shone a light in his eyes. He heard them talking but their alien voices seemed to come from far away and their words did not concern him.

"I don't understand!"

"He was recovering nicely."

"His pulse was normal. His temperature was normal."

"He was back on his feet and well enough to put up a fight."

"It's almost as if he's given up."

"As if he's lost the will to live."

Later, Cloud came. Small Fry recognised her voice but when he opened his eyes he did not know her. They had washed away the smell of her, too. She was a stranger in alien clothes, a dour-faced girl in a lumpy red dress and a green cardigan, not *his* Cloud. When she touched him, he turned away from her. And he heard her beg as Cloud would never have begged.

"Please help him! Please!"

"We have to get him out of here!" Baxter said urgently.

"He's likely to die if we do!" Kate protested.

"He'll die for sure if we don't!" said Baxter.

"How can you possibly know that?"

"He's wild, Kate. Put a wild creature in a cage, shut it away from the sky and land and all that gives it life, and something dies in it."

"I think you're being dangerously romantic, Joel."

"I'm telling you, Kate! He needs to be free!"

"With us," said Cloud.

"Yes," agreed Baxter. "They all need to be free. It's soul-destroying shutting those kids up in that blasted dreary hostel. Deprivation of the worst possible kind!"

"It's only temporary," said Kate.

"Until you can find somewhere better?" asked Baxter. "And what does that mean? Splitting them up? Putting them into foster homes and training schools? Civilising them? That's not what they need! We've civilised our blasted selves until there's nothing natural left in us, so why do it to them? We found out on Earth it wasn't the answer!"

"We didn't come here to live like barbarians, Joel!"

"Maybe not, but we agreed before we colonised this planet that the rights of the native population would be preserved! It's written in the Constitution, Kate! The right to manage their own territories, practise their own religion and adhere to their own way of life! So why treat these kids differently?"

"Because they *are* kids, Joel, and they're under my care!"

"In that case you'll abide by the constitutional guidelines and do what has to be done for them," Baxter said smoothly. "Which means arranging for them to be relocated to a Reservation as soon as possible."

"You really expect me to do that? Dump them in some place they don't even know and leave them to fend for themselves? Is that what you're asking?"

"It's what we want," Cloud said earnestly.

"Meanwhile we'll take this boy out of here,"

Baxter concluded.

"I don't believe this!" said Kate.

Small Fry believed it. The starman had told him he was on his side. His death-wish died and his heartbeat quickened, hammered loudly in his ribcage with an upsurge of hope. Smoothly shaven, and clean and scentless as Cloud, Baxter took off his jacket, put it on Small Fry and lifted him from the bed. His blue eyes twinkled.

"Let's go, Small Fry," he said.

Most of Jasper's Creek was still under construction – all raw earth, steel girders and concrete foundations. But the hostel was complete, sprawling prefabricated buildings within an asphalt compound, set among tyre dumps, motor car repair shops and tin-roofed workshops on a treeless street. It had been built as temporary accommodation for homeless families when the third wave of immigrants arrived from the stars. Now, until the fourth wave of immigrants landed, its buildings were mostly unused, the doors and windows boarded up. Only the reception block remained open, offering shelter and advice to vagrants during the winter months.

In a foyer full of artificial plants in pots, Baxter set Small Fry on his feet. The place had been recently cleaned. Disinfectant disguised the reek of mould and decay, and cooking smells wafted from a nearby kitchen. An overall chill, as yet unalleviated by the central heating, made Small Fry shiver. He would not be staying there for long, the starman promised. And

Kate said the same, although maybe her meaning was different.

An area supervisor, named Mrs Hawkins, took Small Fry in charge. Barefoot into the strangeness, up a flight of concrete stairs and into an area of the building where Cloud was not allowed, he followed her with a sinking heart. The toilets and showers were for men and boys only, she informed him, as was the dormitory, although she did not explain why. In a long narrow room partitioned into cubicles, each containing a bed and a locker, Small Fry was allocated clothes and a space.

"I'll wait while you dress," said Mrs Hawkins.

They were alien clothes, stiff and uncomfortable. The shirt irritated his neck. Hard leather shoes crippled his feet, and the seams of his jeans rubbed the insides of his thighs. He wanted his own clothes, his deerskin skirt and his pouch. But they had gone missing at the infirmary, Mrs Hawkins said, and as he was he looked reasonably presentable.

She led him back the way he had come. Double doors opened from the foyer into a vast room full of tables and chairs, the far end of which had been cleared to make a play area for the children with mats on the floor and boxes of donated toys. The view through the windows was as dull as the sky: an asphalt yard with garbage bins bordered by a chain-link fence, and a construction site beyond where great yellow machines gouged out the soil. It would be wonderful when it was finished, Mrs Hawkins said, a drive-in shopping precinct similar to those they had had on Earth.

Small Fry gazed in dismay. Neon signs flashed on the far horizon and what was wonderful to Mrs Hawkins seemed terrible to him. All he could see was the mutilation of the land that the Great Spirit forbade. And the cloying scent of her perfume made him feel sick.

"Come and join the others," she urged.

His shoes squeaked on the linoleum as he followed her between the tables. Kate, kneeling on the floor among the children, looked up and smiled as he approached. But the children themselves, huddled together and dressed as he was in alien clothes, gazed at him silently, their large purple eyes reflecting his own despair. Brightly-coloured bricks, small replicas of alien machines, tiny totem animals and golden-haired dolls with thrusting breasts, lay strewn around them.

Not knowing what he was supposed to do, Small Fry stood beside Cloud and watched. A volunteer starwoman, younger than Mrs Hawkins, sat on a chair and rocked the baby. Another offered a plastic rattle to the toddlers, shook it gently to create a soft menacing sound ... the sound of the clakka-snake coiled in the grass and about to strike. The youngsters wailed and withdrew, clinging to their siblings for comfort.

"Leave them alone!" Cloud said angrily.

"They need stimulation," Mrs Hawkins explained.

"Not like that!" retorted Cloud.

"So what do you suggest?" Kate asked her.

"Just give them our own things!" said Cloud.

"What things?" asked the younger starwoman.

"Our goats," said Cloud. "And our furs and blankets."

"We can't have goats in here," Kate said gently.

"And the furs were disgusting," said Mrs Hawkins. "They weren't properly cured and they smelled horrible. The same with the blankets. I've put them in the garbage."

"They're ours and we want them!" Cloud insisted.

Mrs Hawkins sighed. "I was hoping you'd co-operate now your boyfriend is here."

"He's not a boy! He's a man!" Cloud retorted.

"He's barely fifteen," protested Mrs Hawkins.

"And we don't want to be here anyway!" Small Fry stated.

"Problems?" said Baxter from behind them.

"Nothing we can't handle," Kate replied. "I'll see what I can do about your belongings," she promised Cloud. "They might be retrievable. And you really won't be here for very long," she said to Small Fry. "We'll be moving you to somewhere more suitable just as soon as we can. There's a child psychiatrist coming next week from Ohio Town to assess your needs."

"Who needs a psychiatrist?" asked Baxter.

"It's standard practice," said Kate.

"There's nothing wrong with these kids bar what they're deprived of! I've made some initial enquiries. There's land available around Tyler's Bluff, and a freight train heading south tomorrow night—"

"I'll bear it in mind," said Kate.

"You'll do more than that," said Baxter. "You'll flaming well fix it! Goats and all!"

"Don't tell me how to do my job!" snapped Kate.

"Would you rather I did it for you?" asked Baxter.

"It's not your place to!" Mrs Hawkins said sharply.

"They're only here because of me!" Baxter reminded her.

"And now they're under the jurisdiction of the Welfare Department," said Mrs Hawkins. "What happens to them in the long term is not up to you or Miss O'Halloran. And if you're going to be abusive about it, I can only suggest you leave!"

Baxter's face was as harsh as his voice. "Very well, if that's how you want it! But don't think that's the end of it!" He glanced at Cloud and Small Fry. "I'll be back," he said. "And that's a promise."

Small Fry nodded, but as Baxter turned and walked away he felt afraid. Under the alien regime of the Jasper's Creek Welfare Department, and the watchful eyes of Kate and Mrs Hawkins and the volunteer starwomen, he and Cloud and the children could be trapped for ever.

Gradually, as the long day wore on, Small Fry realised what was required of him and what was required of them all – total compliance to the starwomen's ways, an unprotesting obedience. But Cloud stayed obstinate and the children failed to understand. Inert and unresponsive, they squatted together on the floor, not knowing they were supposed to catch the ball that was thrown at them, or repeat after Mrs Hawkins the alien words she spoke. And, not knowing they were supposed to wear clothes through all their waking hours, they took them off at every opportunity.

The starwomen struggled to control them. When mealtime came, most children were carried bodily and seated on chairs round the tables. They stared uncomprehendingly at the spoons clutched in their hands and the plates of fish sticks and cabbage that were placed before them. It was food they did not recognise, nor like the smell of, and had no desire to eat. But the starwomen tried to force them. Boys spat and gagged, and the girls wept.

"We can't go on like this!" said Mrs Hawkins.

"So leave them alone!" screeched Cloud.

"They can't not eat," said one of the volunteer women.

"They're nothing but skin and bone as it is," said another.

"They obviously need more time to adapt," said Kate. "They've only been here a few days. Maybe we should feed them on the floor and let them use their fingers?"

"That's not the idea," Mrs Hawkins objected.

Day-long the struggle continued: toilet training, behaviour training, language training, play responses and another meal – a civilised routine guided by a time-mechanism on the wall that Kate called a clock. The restraints and impositions seemed endless. But they had to learn, Mrs Hawkins declared, and it was all for their own good in the end.

When darkness fell, drawn curtains shut out the world. Pictures that Small Fry could make no sense of, flickered on a screen in the corner of the room. And at half-past eight he was marched upstairs with the rest of them, stripped, showered, disinfected, made to dress in pyjamas and put to bed. A nurse sent from the infirmary checked his temperature, changed the bandage on his leg and thrust an antibiotic tablet down his throat. Then the starwoman in charge of the dormitory kissed him on the forehead and Mrs Hawkins switched off the lights.

He lay in the orange darkness listening to the younger boys, each one alone and crying in their separate cubicles. What was natural for the star people was punishment for the children of the Wolf-clan. Only the result of a grave misdemeanour caused them to be cast out from the log-house or their family tents to sleep alone.

Small Fry did what he could to comfort them, had them take off their pyjamas and gather round his bed. Keeping his voice to a whisper, he told them stories Brown Trout had told to him. He told of the naming rites when the soul of a creature merged with the soul of a man and shared its power. He told of the winged karrakeel who dwelled in the caves of shadow beneath Skadhu, and the prophecy of their returning. The karrakeel would save them if Baxter did not, he said. They would unite all the clans, all the hunters and warriors, and lead them back to their own lands again.

After a while he felt the building emptying. Quietly, so as not to alert anyone who lingered, Small Fry left his bed and opened the door. Outside on the concrete landing was a window open to the night, a whiff of freedom. He fetched the boys, fetched Cloud and the girls and the baby, too. Then, naked and together, with only the thin alien blankets to cover them, they sat beneath it breathing in the cold dark air, the thrilling scents of wind and rain, sodden soil and hints of grass. Light from the two moons through breaks in the cloud scurried across their faces – until Kate came to check on them.

Small Fry stared at her in a sudden shock of light. She looked strange and beautiful. Her long blue gown was belted at the waist. Her cheeks were flushed and her tousled hair gleamed with a thousand points of fire. But her green eyes flashed and he could hear the anger in her voice.

"What do you think you're doing?" she snapped.

"We want to be outside," said Cloud.

"It's the middle of the night!" Kate said crossly. "You've got no clothes on and it's freezing! Now get back to bed, all of you!"

No one moved. She slammed the window shut and turned to face them, a group of native children in an alien world where they did not belong. Maybe she saw it in their faces, saw it in their eyes, their need and their longing, their despair at being where they were. Her voice gentled.

"Is it really so bad here?" she asked.

She needed no answer.

"Maybe you can go outside tomorrow," she said.

"Or maybe never," muttered Cloud.

Kate squatted on her heels before them.

"I've found your furs," she said. "I've hung them on the fence for the rain to sweeten them."

"That's not enough," said Cloud.

"We'll run away," vowed Small Fry.

Kate nodded. "OK," she said. "But don't do it tonight. Bear with us, just for one more day, until I can arrange things with Joel."

"You're going to help us?" asked Small Fry.

"Clearly someone has to," said Kate. "But keep it to yourselves. And don't say anything to Mrs Hawkins, or I'll be dismissed. Now, will you try and co-operate? Keep your clothes on, stop crapping in the flower pots, and go back to your beds?"

The hostel stank of furs and blankets drying on the radiators, and throughout another day the children huddled together on the dining-room floor, miserable and apathetic, not understanding what Kate had said the night before. It was secret between Cloud and Small Fry, something they shared in their smiles and their glances, an upsurge of life, a thrill of excitement. They ate because of it and bade the children eat. They kept on their clothes, used the lavatory as they were supposed to and afterwards washed their hands. Mrs Hawkins and the volunteer starwomen were pleased with their progress, rewarding them with sweets and glasses of Coke.

During the afternoon Kate was not there. She returned for hygiene training, the bedtime ritual of soap and showers. Her face gave nothing away. It was composed and expressionless. No confirmation showed in her eyes, no flicker of hope. She had failed, Small Fry thought desperately, and the escape they had planned was not going to happen.

Lying on the bed in his cubicle, listening to the younger boys crying, he wanted to weep with them. But he was a man now and they looked to him as their leader, expected him to be strong. He would wait, he decided, until the building emptied and the cars drove away, find a window that would open and make his own escape. It was the only comfort he could offer them, a return journey across the plains beyond Jasper's Creek, a freedom that would likely kill them.

Later, in the orange darkness, Small Fry made his move, had the boys dress in their alien day-clothes and went to rouse Cloud and the girls. But her trust was stronger than his, the trust of a girl for a woman rooted in some mysterious source within her. Obdurate and scowling, she made her stand. Death was a warrior's option, she declared. No one would choose it who had children to think of, and they were not going anywhere without Kate.

Small Fry was still arguing with her when the truck arrived and Kate and Baxter came upstairs to collect them. Blond-haired in the light, damp from the rain, the starman stood in the doorway. The little ones ran to him and hugged him, instinctively knowing why he was there, and bright tears of joy shone in Cloud's eyes. She had been right all along and Small Fry felt shame for his lack of trust, not of Kate and Baxter but of her.

The starman grinned at him. "Ready for the off, Small Fry?"

"Where're our things?" asked Cloud.

All that was theirs was already loaded in the back of the truck. Goats and familiar smells surrounded them as they made the short journey to the railroad depot. There under the orange soda lights, with a hamper of food and bottles of water, they were transferred to a freight train carrying cattle. It reminded Small Fry of the log-house, a wooden wagon with straw on the floor and scents of the night seeping through the slats – air and animals and rain. With a sigh of relief he stashed their belongings and took his place beside Cloud and the baby. Tired children, happy at last, settled to sleep in their bed of furs. Goats, tethered in the corner, chewed their cud. Sounds from the freight yard and Kate and Baxter talking were carried by the wind through the open doorway.

"I'll bill the Welfare Department," said Kate.

"No need," said Baxter. "I've already paid the fare."

"I thought you were broke?"

"A loan from my brother-in-law," said Baxter.

"What about the truck hire?"

"A loan from Mr Curry's brother-in-law," said Baxter. "He'll pick it up in the morning."

"And you don't need my help on the journey?"

"We managed without you before," Baxter reminded her.

"Nevertheless," Kate reasoned, "it might be best if I came with you. Things might not be that straightforward. There will be forms to fill in, a land claim to register, and I'm used to dealing with officialdom."

"We've already been through this," Baxter said patiently.

"Those kids are my responsibility, too, Joel!"

"You want to become party to their abduction and risk losing your job? I'm giving you a chance, Kate!"

"Thanks," said Kate. "But we haven't time to argue and I prefer to see they're all right."

She and Baxter climbed on board, and the train began to move. Thankful, Small Fry closed his eyes. Vast distances lay ahead, days of travel to an unknown destination, an unknown life, but now he no longer cared where he went, providing it was far away from Jasper's Creek and every place like it.

Throughout the night as Small Fry slept, and throughout the following day, the train sped southwards across the coastal plain. He could see through a knot-hole in the wooden wall of the wagon the grass already greening in the autumn rain. He watched for hours, heedless of the cramped conditions Kate complained of: water dripping through the roof, the smells of goats and dung and urine, bellows of cattle from the adjoining wagons and the permanent semi-darkness.

"It's not meant to be a picnic," Baxter told her.

"I think it's nice," said Cloud.

"How can you *say* that?" Kate asked her.

Small Fry knew why. The wagon was indistinguishable from the world outside, just a single door between them and the open ranch-lands they were passing through. He knew why the children sang. The motion of the freight train was as constant and soothing as the rhythm of its wheels on the rails. They had food and water, their furs to sleep in, and clean draughts whistled through the cracks.

"We like it," Cloud said simply.

"I guess there's no accounting for taste," said Kate.

Next morning, when Small Fry peered through the knot-hole, the scene outside was different. They were passing through a scarred landscape of spoil tips and gravel workings, motorway construction sites and raw new towns until finally, by mid-afternoon, there was no trace left of land itself. It was buried beneath the crowded industrial environs of a mighty city.

"Kennedy," said Kate. "The main space-port."

"Where we star-people first landed," Baxter explained.

The train slowed, stopped for refuelling and the feeding and watering of the cattle. Baxter opened the door. Hazy sunlight touched on the skyscraper blocks beyond the station terminus. A tinny alien voice, announcing the departure of a passenger train, was drowned by the sound of a jet-plane taking off. Like a great silver bird, it veered southwards towards other

73

continents that Small Fry had not known existed.

The children wailed and clutched their ears, but Kate stood in the doorway breathing deeply. Small Fry sniffed warily. Stinks, far more obnoxious than the smells within the wagon, hung in the air and, mingled among them, was another smell, an underlying reek of rot or decay.

Kate wrinkled her nose. "What *is* that pong?"

"Kiku droppings," said Cloud.

"Crowlings to you," said Baxter.

Us, thought Small Fry.

"I've never heard of them," said Kate.

Baxter pointed them out – birds, black as beetles and not much larger, scratching among the ballast beside the railway line, and others beneath the cattle wagons pecking at the dung and urine that seeped through the cracks in the floor. They were classed as carrion-eaters, said Baxter, miniature vultures with toothed bills, but any kind of biodegradable refuse would do, and they were obviously adapting well to city life.

Kate shuddered. "Who wants to visit the washroom?" she asked.

No one did. The youngsters crouched in the shadows, afraid of the noise and sickened by the outside smells. They could live a while longer with their grubby hands and faces, and they had a toilet – an access hatch in the corner which they lifted as necessary. But the supply of food and water needed replenishing and Kate, alone, could not carry everything.

Eventually Baxter stayed with the children and Cloud and Small Fry went with Kate, walked along the tracks to the main station concourse. It was all glass and tiles, a roar of locomotives idling between the platforms, crowds of star-people milling about, strange coloured eyes that stared at them from colourless faces, harsh lights and flashing signs, smells from the fast-food bars and glittering shop fronts. They sat on a red plastic bench and waited while Kate showered in an underground room, then followed her into a nearby department store.

With a wire basket each they wandered among counters displaying a bewildering multitude of alien artefacts – bottles of perfume and bright ceramic pots, postcards of scenes in the city, porcelain statuettes and other more mysterious objects. Cloud found a box covered in plush red fabric that played tinkling music when she lifted the lid. And Small Fry tried on a black felt hat, saw himself reflected from all directions in mirrored pillars that rose towards the ceiling. Closed circuit television cameras showed him walking away with the hat still on his head, and Cloud beside him clutching the box.

Several minutes later, while Kate chose toiletries and an essential change of clothes, they filled their baskets with gifts for the children and were accosted for shoplifting by the store detective. They did not understand about paying for things, Kate explained, when she came to rescue them. Everything they had taken had to be put back, except the hat and music-box which she let them keep.

"I'll buy them for you as a present," she said.

"Why can't you buy the other things as well?" asked Cloud.

"I'm not made of money!" said Kate.

Money, Small Fry discovered, was either metal discs and paper or a cash card. In the alien society it seemed you could have nothing without it, not even food and water or the use of the underground washroom. In banks and factories and high-rise office blocks, in a multitude of ways and places, doing jobs they either liked or hated, the star-people worked throughout their adults lives to earn it. And wages, said Kate as they passed through the checkout, were never enough.

Laden with sandwiches and bottled drink, Cloud's music-box and Kate's new clothes, they walked back along the track.

"Why don't you all live as we do?" Cloud asked her.

"It's not our way," said Kate.

"*Our* way is better," said Cloud. "We live from what the land provides, and everything else we make and give."

"Or exchange for what others make," said Small Fry.

Kate kicked at the crowlings among the stones. "You sound like Joel," she said crossly. "But given a choice, how many would willingly do without modern conveniences and live in a tent? To most of us star-people that would be a descent into barbarism and we stopped killing each other a long time ago. Or have you forgotten why you're here?"

Cloud and Small Fry glanced at each other. They had not forgotten, nor would they ever forget. All they knew and remembered would be handed on to succeeding generations. And no matter what Kate and the star-people believed, they had to stay true to themselves and each other, the souls of their ancestors and their native ways.

Cloud glanced at his hat.

Small Fry glanced at her musical jewellery box.

"Why did we want them?" he asked.

"To remind us that we don't?" she said.

They laughed together, gales of laughter that mingled with the noises of the alien city they would soon be leaving and never wanted to see again. Kate frowned. The locomotive driver, and a gang of starmen in grimy coveralls working on the track, turned to stare at them. They did not know what Cloud and Small Fry had discovered ... that it was good to be themselves in spite of all they had lost.

For another night, another day, they journeyed southwards. The weather grew warmer, the hours of sunlight increased as if they had left the approaching winter behind and returned to summer. Sun beat down on the roof of the wagon and the inside air grew hot and stifling. There was barely a breeze, even with the door wide open. Baxter discarded his shirt, the children their clothes, and Kate's red hair was damp with sweat, although Small Fry kept his hat on.

The land beyond Kennedy City had been green and lush with semi-tropical vegetation. A playground of the rich, Baxter remarked. He was jealous, Kate had said. But it was she who desired the sailing boats and speed boats and white villas crouching on the shores of blue lakes, thought Small Fry. And when they crossed the Arizona river, the land displayed a greater richness Kate failed to see.

It was bleak and awful, she said. But Small Fry gazed at it in awe, and its richness grew as the train approached Tyler's Bluff. No child stayed untouched, except the baby who slept oblivious. Their eyes shone. Their chatter grew shrill with excitement, and Cloud had no need to tell them to put on their clothes. Wild and free, the land beyond the doorway that would soon be theirs called to their souls. Even the goats seem to sense it, bleating and stamping and tugging at their leashes, impatient to arrive.

"Not long now," promised Baxter.

"It can't be yet," Kate protested.

Baxter glanced at his watch. "Another half-hour," he said. "Fifty more miles perhaps?"

Kate laughed in relief. "I thought for a moment you meant this was it."

Time, however, and a few more miles made little difference to the passing landscape. They alighted at sundown at a wayside halt, stood together in the sand and dust clutching their few belongings and watched the train pull away. Carrying the cattle on to their deaths in the cities of the southern seaboard, the clatter of its wagons and the noise of its wheels on the track gradually faded into a bliss of quiet.

The day was still warm, the baked earth shimmering with heat, although the air was dry and clear. For a while no one spoke. It was as if they drank of the place with their ears and eyes, space and silence as vast as the sky and the desert around them, all rose and gold and purple with shadows. And within it there was life and sounds. A soft wind set the leaves of the thorn-briars dancing, sang around the rock-stacks and pinnacles, and touched their faces with the coolness of the coming night. Crag-hawks wheeled around the flat-topped cliffs of the bluff, and amber-eyed mikklau, sand-lizards in Baxter's language, basked in the evening sunlight on red weathered rocks beside the railroad track. A colony of goupa grazed on a patch of sparse grass nearby, and a blue flax flower bloomed among the stones at Cloud's feet.

She put down the marriage tent and bent to pick it, and Small Fry understood the meaning in her eyes. It was loincloths to her, a way of making clothes, and the goupa and mikklau were not just meat but stretched skins, leather for moccasins and hunting pouches and a thousand other things. Her grin confirmed what Small Fry already knew: they could survive in that land between them. But Kate's voice was scathing.

"Are you mad, Joel?"

"Pardon?" said Baxter.

"You heard me!" Kate said furiously.

"What have I done?" asked Baxter.

"You really need to ask? Look around you, for Christ's sake! There's nothing here! And you expect these children to live on their own in a place like this? You must be out of your mind!"

Baxter spread his hands. "Given a choice I would hand this whole world back to them and ship us out of it. Only it's not up to me. This is all we allow them, Kate, swamps and deserts and tundra, land that is no use to us. And if you think that's unjust, don't complain to me, take it up with the politicians."

He shouldered his travel bag and strode up a rocky incline towards the bluff, following the tracks of tyres in the dust. Cloud and Small Fry, goats and children, a girl carrying the baby, and the screech of Kate's voice, trailed behind him.

"I should never have listened to you! I should never have let you take them away from Jasper's Creek! You lied, Joel! You deliberately deceived me! You said they would be better off on a Reservation! But what kind of life will they have here? At least if they'd stayed with the Welfare Department we could have provided them with a decent, civilised existence!"

"What's she talking about?" asked Cloud.

"Hats and music-boxes," said Small Fry.

"Just ignore her," Baxter advised.

The length of his stride increased. The children had almost to run to keep up with him and Cloud, with the music-box under her arm and dragging the marriage tent, stirred up the dust. Iron-red cliffs towered before them, and echoes of Kate mingled with the mewling cries of the crag-hawks.

"You won't get away with this, Joel! I shall file a report! And don't think I'm staying here to give you a hand! You're on your own now! Do you hear me?"

Twilight deepened as they topped the rise, and Kate was on her own, left behind and shouting for them to wait, her anger replaced by fear. She feared what Cloud, Small Fry and the children loved and needed, what Baxter chose: the land itself and all that lived with it – day-creatures and night-creatures, flittermice and fox cries and the sudden angry rattle of a clakka-snake.

It uncoiled from its nest of grass as Kate came running to rejoin them, its fangs poised to strike. But with a wild cry Cloud dropped the tent and pushed her aside. Small Fry leapt, deftly caught the snake by its tail, swung it round and smashed its head against a rock. It writhed feebly and Kate stared at it, her face gone pale as the first moon rising.

"*Now* do you doubt their abilities to survive?" asked Baxter.

She shook her head.

"Clakkas make good eating," Cloud informed her.

That one made a meal for the kiku scurrying from their roosts in a nearby gully, drawn by its death throes or the smell of its blood. Small Fry squatted on his heels to watch them, tiny birds he detested and denied. Moonlight sheened their feathers and their dark eyes glittered, bright with life.

They were not death-birds, he realised. All that was dead or foul they converted into living energy, the warmth of their own blood, their own fecundity. Kiku would survive whatever their circumstances, as the clan who bore their name would survive, and they were not without purpose either. Toothed beaks pecked and cleansed and the planet was sweeter for their existence. Suddenly, Small Fry was not ashamed to share their name. He was not ashamed to be Crowling.

"Can we go?" Kate asked shakily.

"Whenever you're ready," said Baxter.

She set her face towards the bluff. "Why didn't you tell me there was a Reception Centre here?"

"I assumed you knew," said Baxter. "Every Reservation has one, with food stores, farm stores, fodder supplies and various other facilities. It's part of the relocation package. Tag along and you can even take a shower." He tipped the black felt hat over Small Fry's eyes. "Coming, Small Fry?"

The boy rose to his feet, looked up at the starman from under its brim. "Crowling," he said. "Not Small Fry."

"Pardon?" said Baxter.

"It's who I really am," said Crowling.

"*That's* your man-name?" Cloud said sharply.

"Yes," said Crowling.

"Well, well," murmured Baxter. "Now *there's* a turn up for the books. Abu-ben-Crowling, may his tribe increase..."

"It's a good name," Cloud said stoutly.

Crowling glanced at her. "You really think so?" he asked.

She nodded emphatically and her plump hand

sought his, squeezed his fingers reassuringly. "I like it," she declared. "It means our clan will survive no matter what happens."

Baxter chuckled. "I don't doubt that," he agreed. "Luppas, bakkaus and ice-bears might become extinct, and so might we, but crowlings will go on for ever. This planet could be yours again after all, one day."

"Would someone kindly explain what's going on?" asked Kate.

"Stick around and you might find out," Baxter informed her. "And as clan chief you'll need to be registered," he told Crowling. "Two names they insist upon, forename and surname. So what's it to be? John Crowling? Small-Fry Crowling?"

"Ben," Cloud said promptly. "Abu-ben-Crowling ... like you just said."

"Done!" said Baxter.

Ben Crowling nodded his agreement and straightened his hat. A man now, and proud of his name, he walked beside the starman towards the buildings and the Reservation. Cloud and Kate and the children followed, driving the goats, carrying the baby, carting the baggage.

"Hey!" shouted Kate. "Give us a hand, you two!"

Baxter grimaced, then turned to obey her, but under the sky and the moons and the desert stars, Ben Crowling continued on his way. Shifting camp was women's work still and he let Cloud do it. Plain and plump and strong as a hump-ox, dragging the marriage tent and her own twisted foot, she waddled behind him. It was his way of loving her, respecting her and acknowledging her worth, a kind of deference the star-people had forgotten. And Cloud in her compliance loved and respected him, ruled him for the rest of his days without him knowing.

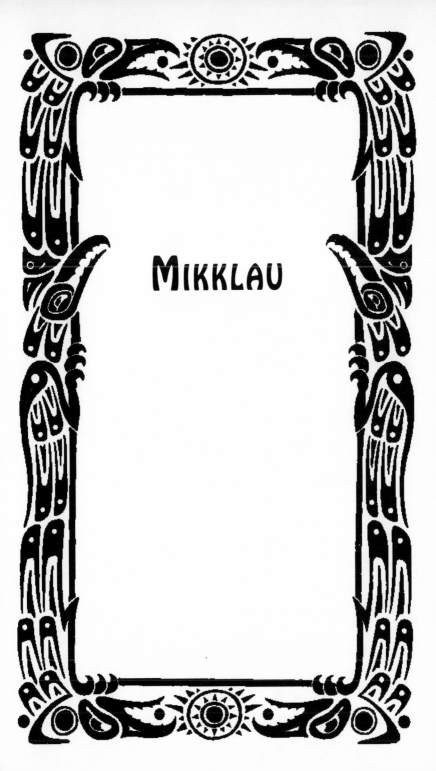

MIKKLAU

Mikklau was roused from his bed of furs by the digital bleep of James Baxter's wristwatch. Shivering in the pre-dawn chill, he dragged a woven blanket round his shoulders and positioned himself where he should have been all night, awake and watchful beneath the goat-skin awning. The moons had set. The wind was icy and the land was sheened with frost. Its cold struck upwards from the ground beneath him.

It was time Mikklau became a man, Grandfather Ben had declared. Time he made his run and found his adult name. It was an old tribal custom and for reasons of his own Mikklau went along with it, up to a point. Being isolated from the clan was no great hardship. It was one way of avoiding Grandmother Cloud and the endless round of chores he had to do. But no way would he deprive himself of food and sleep for three whole days and nights when he did not have to ... and no way was he going to marry Rhawna.

It was not the principle of an arranged marriage that Mikklau objected to. With so many of the Crowling clan inter-related, he understood the need for careful genealogical selection. It was the fact that Grandmother Cloud had offered him no other option that rankled. She could have purchased a bride for him at the next great gathering, a Hump-ox girl or a girl from the Bison clan, but she refused even to consider it. For Mikklau it had to be a Crowling girl – Rhawna, descendant of a former chief, her clan-blood pure as his own – regardless of her looks, her age, or her demeanour.

At ten years old Rhawna was nothing but a child, buck-toothed and goggle-eyed as a goupa, and thin as the winter's twig after which she was named. Mikklau rebelled against the very idea of taking her to wife. He rebelled against his grandmother, too, and the pointless ritual he was now involved in. Running on an empty stomach until he dropped would not make a man of him and, no matter what creature he happened upon, his name would not change. He had been registered as Mikklau Crowling at the Records Office and, officially, he would be Mikklau Crowling for the rest of his days.

Scowling, he pulled the blanket tighter round him and watched the sun rise, Gamma Centauri touching the peaks of the South Sierras and gilding the desert around him with orange-gold light. Rock-stacks and pinnacles, cliffs and canyons and the distant hump of Tyler's Bluff glowed with fiery hues, although the settlement below remained in shadow. The small adobe houses, built among the ruins of a once great city, seemed to sleep as the land awoke.

"Hurry up!" he muttered.

Slowly the night's cold receded. Dawn flowers, dampened by melting frost, opened their petals and briefly bloomed, their massed colours carpeting the hillsides in clumps of blue and mauve and crimson. Barrel-crickets chirred among the stones. Crag-hawks left their roosts on the ledges of cliffs and sailed the thermals on lazy wings, and long-legged skooa squabbled in the stand of moth-willow trees on the river bank. Salt flats on the south horizon glittered crystalline white.

After a while Mikklau discarded his blanket. Nearby a freckled sand-lizard, whose name he bore, crawled from the crevice of a ruined wall to seek the growing warmth, and in the settlement below there were signs of life. Smoke of cooking-fires curled upwards from the chimneys to be caught by the ceaseless wind and carried away. Dark-haired children released the fowls from their coops. Goat-herders drove the flock towards the mountains and Ella Baxter headed for the river with a basket of washing. As the shadow-line shifted, Old Ben, Mikklau's grandfather, took up his customary seat on a bench in the sun.

Mikklau's stomach, unattended to since the evening before, curdled with hunger. "Hurry up!" he repeated.

It was the last day of fasting, the last day he would sit alone on the ridge, outcast and ignored – except by James detouring behind him. Hidden by the ruined wall and silent as a native, only the slip of a stone and the rustle of a plastic shopping carrier alerted Mikklau to his presence although, in full view of the settlement, he neither moved nor turned his head.

"What kept you?" he hissed.

"Be grateful I'm here at all!" James retorted.

"No one suspects, do they?"

"You know my grandmother," said James.

All his life Mikklau had known Kate Baxter. When his mother died at his birth she had shared the raising of him: an alien woman, with hair red as fire, dandling him on her knee. She had told him stories of the world among the stars from which she came and taught him her language. He knew the love that had kept her at the settlement despite her longing to live among her own kind. He knew the loss she bore when her son went away to university, her grief at his death in an automobile accident, her devastation when Joel Baxter died. She might have left then, but Ella brought James to the Reservation, a young wife alone with her child seeking the sanctuary and solace her own family failed to provide.

That had been five years ago. Now Ella worked weekends in a gift shop in Tyler's Bluff. James and Mikklau had grown as close as brothers and Kate's affections were shared between them.

"She's nowhere near as bad as Grandmother Cloud," Mikklau said stoutly.

"Not much gets past her though," James reminded him.

"This is the last time anyway," said Mikklau.

"It's what happens afterwards that worries me," said James.

"I shall be well clear by then," Mikklau assured him.

"And I'll have to face the grilling!" said James.

"You're not bound to admit you helped me."

"Where else would you have got the money?" asked James.

Mikklau frowned. He could have stolen it, maybe? Helped himself from the red velvet trinket box Grandmother Cloud kept beneath the bed. Taken a portion of the income she had saved over the decades from the sale of surplus goats and chickens and the occasional artefact. The money, used to purchase wives for young men luckier than Mikklau and ensure the future of the clan, could have ensured a future for himself – except that he would not do that. No Crowling would steal from a cache that belonged to them all.

"How much did you get?" he asked guiltily.

"Fifty dollars," said James. "An advance on next month's pocket money and twenty dollars from my mother's purse. It should get you as far as Kennedy, if you're still determined to go."

There was a moment of silence. Singing sand-larks spiralled up the sky and down below men buried faeces in the bean-fields. They had been hunter-gatherers once in the forests of the north but, unlike most of the clans, under Joel Baxter's guidance they had made the transition to subsistence farming. Created from the desert sand by dung and toil, the small walled paddocks grew what food they needed. All else was manufactured by the labour of their hands, an unending struggle to survive that Mikklau despised.

It did not have to be that way. As did the Hump-ox and Bison, they could have danced for dollars, mass-produced their native arts and crafts for wholesale trade in the alien cities, or sold their labour. They could have bought their clothes from the department store, have flush toilets and televisions and cars. But Grandfather Ben was a stickler for tradition and Grandmother Cloud stood by him. Nor, for all the years she had dwelt among them, could Kate Baxter sway them into accepting any aspect of ease or convenience enjoyed by her own people.

Unlike her husband, Kate had never fully adopted the native way of life. She wore blue jeans, cooked on a bottle-gas stove, drove a pick-up and shopped in town. At her insistence their son had been sent from the Reservation to be educated and James attended the school in Tyler's Bluff.

Soon James, too, would be going away to boarding college and in time would choose the kind of life he wanted, a well-paid career and an air-conditioned apartment in a town or city. But Mikklau, apart from his fluency in the alien language and whatever else Kate and James and Ella had taught him, was virtually illiterate, fitted for nothing but a continuation of what he had been born to: poverty and hardship and obedience to the wishes of his elders ... a lifetime of goat-herding, skinning sand-lizards and setting fish-traps with his father.

The sun climbed higher and the dry wind sang through the ruins. He could feel the carved stones hard against his back, could see in his mind's eye the hieroglyphs linking the past to the present: luppa and bakkau, ice-bear and fire-eagle, and the winged karrakeel. When the karrakeel rose from their tomb beneath Skadhu all the native clans would be united, or so the legend said. And the Crowlings believed it. They looked for salvation to some fabulous winged being as wave upon wave of immigrants arrived from the stars and laid claim to the planet.

Hump-ox and Bison adapted, took what they could from the ones who took everything, but Crowlings refused. They refused to accept that their way of life was obsolete and the Great Spirit in whom they trusted had been superseded by an alien God – a God of autos and billboards, concrete motorways and high-rise apartment blocks, chain-stores and dollars. One day, thought Mikklau, the Crowling clan would become as extinct as the karrakeel if they did not soon wake up and face reality.

Behind the wall the carrier bag rustled.

"Are you listening?" asked James.

"What?" said Mikklau.

"I asked if you really intend to go through with this?"

"I've got to do something!" Mikklau said desperately. "I can't stay here for the rest of my life!"

"There are worse places than this," James informed him. "You know why my mother brought me here. It's a rat-race everywhere else."

"So why are *you* going?" Mikklau asked.

"College is different," said James. "But what are *you* qualified for? Now the seventh wave of immigrants have arrived you'll be competing for every job going. You'll be lucky if you end up washing dishes! Better stay here, if you know what's good for you."

Mikklau bit back his retort. Down below Grandmother Cloud waddled across the compound, unmistakable even from that distance away. Fat and ferocious in her fringed leather skirt, she glanced towards the awning under which he was sitting. He could feel her gaze, sharp as a crag-hawk's, checking that all was as it should be and missing nothing. When Grandmother Cloud was around no one stepped out of line. She ruled the clan as she ruled her husband, except that Grandfather Ben never knew it. But she was less covert with Mikklau. Bringing him up in place of his own mother, she had seldom spared him from the clout of her hand or the venomous lash of her tongue.

"Think about it," James said earnestly. "It's not too late to change your mind. One day you'll be clan chief and able to do as you like. But go to Kennedy or anywhere else and you'll be just one more purple-eyed skivvy."

"Shut it!" said Mikklau.

"It's true!" said James. "My kind don't care a damn about your kind, not really."

"Pass me that shopping carrier!"

Down in the compound Grandmother Cloud cupped her hands. Her voice bellowed on the wind. "Are you talking to someone up there?"

"No!" shouted Mikklau.

"I'm off," James said hurriedly. "The carrier's here, behind the wall. The money's in the bottom and there's food enough for a couple of days. See you this evening. And you never solve anything by running away."

Stones rattled as he slid back down the ridge and below, in the compound with her hands on hips, Grandmother Cloud waited a few moments longer until Kate came to join her. Small and frail beside the native woman's massive bulk, her skin pale in contrast and her red hair faded to grey, she leaned on a walking stick and followed Cloud's gaze.

Grey-green eyes fixed on Mikklau, then scanned along the ridge. Acknowledging the Crowling clan's determination to preserve their native way of life, Kate would not take kindly to those who cheated on tradition. And maybe she guessed what James and Mikklau were doing? Maybe she had found things missing from her refrigerator ... cheese and bread and chocolate bars and several cans of Coke? To the Great Spirit he no longer believed in, Mikklau began to pray.

His prayers were answered. Wherever James was he stayed unseen and the two women turned away, headed towards the house on the edge of the settlement where Mikklau and Rhawna would dwell. Later, when children arrived, additional rooms would be added but for now it was just a single chamber of raw adobe bricks containing a hearth and sleeping shelf, its walls plastered inside and out with river-bed mud and whitened by lime. Within its confines, with a skinny tongue-tied child-wife, Mikklau would be imprisoned – unless he made good his escape.

Shrill girlish giggles, carried by the wind when Grandmother Cloud opened the door, ceased as she and Kate stepped inside. They were home-making, Mikklau supposed, hanging the drapes and tapestries, spreading the rugs and arranging the bed-blankets. And when Rhawna grew she would rule him as all native women ruled their men. With the warmth of her body and food from her hearth she would create a dependency. Or worse still, behind her downcast eyes and unassuming demeanour could lurk another Grandmother Cloud, a tyrant he would have to defer to or suffer the consequences, her every act of servitude a sham.

Mikklau's determination hardened. And behind him the shopping carrier rustled.

James was still there, he thought.

"It's all right for you!" he said bitterly. "You're not being fobbed off with a stupid buck-toothed kid for a wife! If it was Sheranie, I might consider it. But who, in their right mind, would want to marry Rhawna?"

The carrier rustled and James made no reply.

"Would *you*?" Mikklau demanded. "Would you agree to marry her if you were me? I bet you wouldn't! And I shall be a man after tonight! An adult member of the clan, for whatever that's worth! I ought to be allowed to make my own decisions instead of doing what Grandmother Cloud decides!"

The wind whined. Dry grasses beat their heads distractedly and the day's heat shimmered over the distant salt-flats. Oblivious to everything, Grandfather

Ben dozed on his seat, his old felt hat shading his eyes from the sun.

"And don't tell me it was his idea!" Mikklau went on. "He may have decreed it but Grandmother Cloud dreamed it up. He can't even fart without her telling him to! And the same goes for my father and the rest of the men! Your grandfather was the only man I ever knew who wasn't under the thumb. He was an independent spirit, James, beholden to no one. And that's what I want to be."

The wind seemed to mourn. There was an ache in Mikklau's memory and a tombstone by the river bearing Joel Baxter's name. Without him the Crowling clan would not have survived, neither the long trek from the forests of the north nor the shift to a new way of life. Ideas, both native and alien, had mingled in Joel and they warred in Mikklau because of him.

"Do you blame me?" he asked. "It's all very well to preach the good of the clan but what about the individual? I don't want to stay here and breed babies! I want out!"

Girls giggled as Kate and Grandmother Cloud left his and Rhawna's wedding quarters. Their eyes were on him, grey-green and purple, equally suspicious. He could smell bread baking for his naming feast, stretched skins being tanned for leather, the scents of bean-flowers and dust. He could smell, when the shopping carrier rustled, a whiff of decay.

"James?" hissed Mikklau.

"Are you talking to someone?" shouted Grandmother Cloud.

"No!" yelled Mikklau.

And walking beside his mother, come from the direction of the river and carrying a basket of wet washing, James appeared in the compound. Whoever it was behind the wall it was certainly not *him*. With everyone watching, Mikklau crawled from beneath the awning, leapt to his feet and scrambled through an archway where once a window had been.

The smell was stronger now, a vile fetid odour of rotting meat, of something putrefying and dead, although whatever was inside the shopping carrier was obviously alive. Kiku ... kiku ... the white plastic bag heaved and twittered, exploded when he kicked it. Birds, small and black as dung beetles, scurried in all directions. And when he picked up the bag it was empty, except for the tatters of a packet of fries, silver paper from a chocolate bar wrapping, a pecked plastic Coke bottle and fifty dollars in change. That night Mikklau would run on an empty stomach after all.

"Blasted thieving crowlings!" he howled.

When the sun set in a sky of fire, once again Mikklau draped the blankets round his shoulders. Starving and shivering and bored from doing nothing, he waited as his father came up the steep path and placed a laden platter at his feet. An aroma of peppered fish set his stomach churning and, for a third time, Skooa posed the question.

"Will you eat, my son, and live beneath my roof?"

"I'm willing if you are," Mikklau replied.

"You're supposed to refuse!" Skooa said sternly.

"After three days without food I'll agree to anything, Pop."

"Don't give me that!" said Skooa. "The whole clan knows someone's been rifling Kate Baxter's fridge!"

"How could it have been me?" Mikklau demanded. "I've been sitting here in full sight of everyone, except when I went behind the wall to relieve myself."

"You and young James are both old enough to understand these rituals are not without purpose! Separation from the parent needs to be symbolised in many ways! Age alone does not make you a man!"

"It does in alien culture," argued Mikklau.

"You are not an alien, boy!"

"No," Mikklau agreed bitterly. "I'm a primitive in comparison and denied any chance of bettering myself."

"Are their ways better?" Skooa questioned. "Joel Baxter thought not. Your grandparents, too, from their own experience. It is why we live as we do. The Great Spirit is with us and maybe tonight, when you make your run and your soul is bonded to some wild creature, you will know it."

"It sounds like a load of old rope to me," muttered Mikklau.

Skooa picked up the platter. Red-ochre earth stained his fingers and the patterns painted on his short leather skirt had faded from years of wear. Since the woman who had loved and clad and fed him died at Mikklau's birth, Skooa's life had been hard. While other men fished away the afternoons and jawed in the smoke-house until late into the night, Skooa had to fend for himself and tend his own patch of land. He had to kowtow to Grandmother Cloud for help to bring up his son. His reward might have been pride in his achievement, but his voice sounded sad as if he sensed what Mikklau intended.

"You're our future," he said. "Don't shame us, my son, or turn your back on our ways. When the karrakeel rise, and the alien civilisation crumbles and fails, the world will be ours once again. We must not lose sight of how to live."

"You really believe that?" scoffed Mikklau.

"It is all there is to believe," answered Skooa quietly.

He turned away, headed back down the path, and Mikklau bit his lip against an upsurge of guilt. Ever since James had come to live on the Reservation he had been torn between the conflict of his own desires and the beliefs of the clan, their blindness to any other alternative. Even on a practical level he failed to understand them. How could the daily chore of burying the contents of the lavatory bucket be preferred to flush toilets? And why walk thirty miles to the annual gathering dragging their surplus goods for trade when they could drive a car and trailer? Why let their infants and old people die when alien medicine could save them? And why have Mikklau remain ignorant when he could have gone with James to the school in Tyler's Bluff? Their denial made him angry, the anger comforted him, drove away his guilt. If they were to have any future he was right to leave!

Only that way, through competition within the alien society, could the native clans hope to regain their planet.

Frosty stars, incredibly bright, shone in the overhead sky and northwards and eastwards the two moons rose. Below in the small adobe houses, women closed the shutters and settled the children to sleep, although in the compound the black moving shapes of men began to gather. The fire was kindled, bright sparks blowing skywards as the drums began to beat.

Dressed in ritual robes they came to escort him, kinsmen, clansmen to whom he would soon cease to belong. Eyes glinted in the moons' light from masked faces – crag-hawk and goupa, lizard and clakka-snake, scaled eel and catlin fish, Skarrow the shaman with a necklace of crowling skulls around his neck. Tambourines jangled. Flutes carved from moth-willow made a wild music, and Skooa's feather mantle fluttered in the wind as Mikklau descended the ridge.

Too old and slow to make the journey, Grandfather Ben waited within the circle of firelight, a small beaked figure wearing his battered hat, and James stood tall in the darkness beyond him, his fair hair slicked with sweat. As an outsider, James could have no part in the ritual. He was there as an observer, just as Joel Baxter had always been, but his watchful presence made Mikklau uneasy.

Drums beat to the rhythm of his heart as he accepted the shaman's draught. The brew was bitter, its aftermath warming his vitals, intoxicating his brain. He knew then why the naming ritual had such a profound effect on its participants. After three days of isolation and starvation each one in turn was either drugged or drunk. As he began to dance Mikklau felt the world spinning around him, saw the sky revolving full of stars and sparks.

He lost all sense of time and direction. Yet somewhere inside his head was another Mikklau aware of the idiocy of it all. And when the music finally stopped and the mad sounds began of men believing they were insects or animals, fish or fowl, that other Mikklau stayed unperturbed, knowing full well who each masked figure was. He could have denounced them all for their gross stupidity but the Mikklau within him grasped the opportunity that would never come again and urged him to run as he was supposed to do.

Dodging Skooa in his feather mantle, the masks of goupas and desert-foxes, fish-faces and bird-faces and clawed hands that reached out to hold him, and ignoring James's wave of farewell, he sped from the compound and headed into the darkness.

After a while his eyes adjusted. He saw the salt-flats on the horizon glittering in the moonlight and realised he was running in the wrong direction. But the Mikklau that possessed him drove him on, his bare feet in the sand setting a false trail for more than a mile. His footsteps ended where the ruined city ended as he climbed a wall. Following the parapets, where the night wind scoured the stones and removed the dust, he doubled back and returned to the ridge where he had spent the last three days. There, from a secret crevice known only to himself, he retrieved the fifty dollars James had given him. Down in the compound, seen through the broken arch of a window, the men of the Crowling clan danced on but Mikklau would never be one of them. By morning he would reach the railroad station at Tyler's Bluff and it would be two full days before anyone, apart from James, realised he had gone.

Built between the entrance to the Reservation and the railroad track, the town of Tyler's Bluff sprawled along the base of the cliffs. It was dependent upon tourism and small-time mining, shops selling copper and silver-ware, semi-precious gemstones and ethnic arts and crafts. People, both native and alien, mingled in the Saturday street-market and haggled for wares. Bison warriors in their massive head-dresses danced for the crowds in the central square. In quieter streets groups of Hump-ox girls offered their services ... but not to Mikklau. Minus a money pouch he had no means to pay them and they could tell from his loincloth he was not yet a man.

Tired and footsore after a thirty-mile trek, faint from hunger and clutching the fifty dollars tightly in his hand, Mikklau made for the travel depot on the far edge of town. Cars sweltered in the parking lot outside the supermarket. Motels and gas-stations, fast-food restaurants and newly-built housing lots lined the highway beside the railroad track. A streamlined inter-city bus headed south from the depot and the train for Kennedy was leaving the station as Mikklau arrived.

He heard the announcement when he entered the foyer and saw, through the glass doors opposite, the train pull out. Had he run he might have caught it, but a tide of incoming passengers barred his way. Native boys, much of an age with himself, mingled among them and offered to carry their suitcases, touted luck-stones at inflated prices or openly begged for dollars.

Bewildered by the noise and movement, Mikklau waited until the foyer emptied and the boys and their victims were gone. He was alone then in the air-conditioned silence. Vending and ticket machines were abandoned. Floor tiles were cool beneath his naked feet and an overhead computer screen, listing the day's arrivals and departures, informed him there was not another train or bus going to Kennedy until the evening.

His stomach gurgled and automatic doors opened to admit him to the single platform. That, too, was empty except for a bearded vagrant dozing on a red plastic bench in the shade of the overhang. Weary and dispirited, Mikklau sat on a bench nearby, opened his fist to stare at the money and wondered what to do now. He could go south, perhaps, on the midday train to one of the cities on the southern seaboard, or take a bus, which would be cheaper. In either case he needed food and drink. Burger smells wafted on the wind from the drive-in restaurant on the highway. How much would it cost him? he wondered. And how long would a burger and a can of Coke satisfy his hunger and thirst?

Seated in the shadow of the roof-awning, he felt the day's heat building up, saw it shimmering above the steel rails of the track. Northwards the train for Kennedy had faded into distance and southwards, where the highway crossed the track, the barrier had lifted. A signal glowed red to warn the oncoming trains. Dust and thorn-briar drifted in the wind, and the scent of fries and burgers was almost overwhelming. The fifty dollars jingled in Mikklau's hand.

Hearing it, the vagrant stirred. Coughing and spitting, he rose to his feet, shouldered the canvas haversack he had used as a pillow and came lurching towards the bench where Mikklau was sitting. As if unaware of the heat, he wore a woollen hat and scarf and tattered overcoat, and heavy leather boots that made scuff marks on the surface of the concrete. Vivid blue eyes, fixed firmly on the hand that held the money, finally shifted to meet Mikklau's own.

"Can you spare a few dollars?" he asked.

His voice was slurred, and the neck of a whiskey bottle protruded from his overcoat pocket.

"No, I can't," Mikklau said curtly.

"Ah, come on," wheedled the vagrant. "You've had a better morning's begging than I have, that's for sure. And I've had nothing to eat since the day before yesterday."

"You and me both," said Mikklau. "And I'm not a beggar."

"You're native, though," said the vagrant.

"What if I am?" Mikklau demanded.

"So if you ain't a beggar you must be a thief or a bum-seller. But it's no odds to me. Just give me a couple of dollars and I'll not report you. That a deal, is it?"

"No!" Mikklau said hotly. "I'm none of those things so there's nothing to report. Go away and leave me alone!"

The vagrant hesitated for a moment, then sat on the seat beside him. He smelt of drink and unwashed clothes, and among the grey of his beard and brows were traces of red. His hair was red, too, the same as Kate's had been, only long and matted. Mikklau could not guess how old he was. Dried burrs of barley grass stuck to the bottle-green wool of his hat.

"I seen how much you've got in your hand," he said pointedly.

"Enough for the fare to Kennedy," agreed Mikklau.

The vagrant raised an eyebrow. "Ain't you one of the local tribes from the Reservation?"

"Yes," said Mikklau.

"So what do you want to go to Kennedy for? Ain't nothing there for the likes of you. Do yourself a favour and go on home."

Mikklau frowned. The man had no idea but it was one way to be rid of him. "Maybe I will," he said.

"Very wise of you," said the vagrant. "Kennedy's no place for a young boy on his own. And as you won't be needing the money any more you can spare me some. Two dollars fifty for a cheese shandwich, maybe?"

106

Mikklau unclenched his fist. The coins James had given him winked in the light and the vagrant's grimy palm spread to receive them. Feeling he had no choice, Mikklau selected two dollars fifty and placed it in the callused hand.

"Here!" he said angrily. "Take it and go!"

In a moment of silence the vagrant pocketed the money and rose to leave. Along the highway a convoy of trucks rumbled southwards towards the railroad crossing and faint and far away a locomotive whistled, the sound of it funnelled through Deep Rock Canyon and across the flats.

"That's my train," remarked the vagrant.

"So don't let me keep you," muttered Mikklau.

"What about you?" asked the vagrant.

"What about me?" Mikklau demanded.

"You'll be returning to the Reservation, will you?"

"Not necessarily," Mikklau said coldly.

"Still off to Kennedy, are we?"

"If I am," said Mikklau, "it's nothing to do with you!"

He stared down the track. The whistle of the train was nearer now, and the road barriers lowered as the signal changed to green. The vagrant clicked his tongue.

"Never let it be said I didn't warn you," he announced. "But if you must go there you'd best come with me. We can board this oncoming train and be there by dark."

Mikklau gazed at him, and his heartbeat quickened. The slur was gone from the vagrant's voice and the bearded face was younger than he'd thought. The blue eyes seemed softened with a strange concern.

"What do you mean?" Mikklau demanded.

"What I've just said," replied the vagrant.

"But I thought there wasn't another train to Kennedy until this evening."

"You thought wrong then," said the vagrant. "There are two freight-trains a day and one at night, empty cattle wagons going all the way north to Jasper's Creek. Have you never been freight-hopping, boy?"

"No," said Mikklau.

"No need for a ticket, see?" the vagrant informed him. "Just a walk down the track, raise the road barrier and have the crossing lights switch to red, then on we get. And when she stops in Kennedy to refuel we get off again. You with me, are you?"

Eagerly, Mikklau rose to his feet. "Do you really mean it?"

The vagrant nodded. "J. Samuel Hoddle's my name," he said. "But you can call me Sam. Where's your luggage, boy?"

"I haven't got any," said Mikklau.

"You can't walk round Kennedy looking like that," said Sam.

"Why not?" asked Mikklau.

"Don't you know nothing about propriety?" asked Sam, as they set off together along the track.

The locomotive slowed and stopped, and when the

guard left the box-van to investigate, Sam and Mikklau slipped from the shelter of a billboard and climbed on board. It was an empty cattle wagon they were in, shadowy and sunless and reeking of disinfectant, its floors still damp from sluicing. They could hear shouting along the track and see through the slats when the guard returned. Road traffic had halted at the barrier when the train moved off.

It was the last Mikklau saw of Tyler's Bluff, dust in the sunlight and red cliffs sliding by, neon signs along the highway and a whiff of fries and burgers. Then the desert took over and the high wire fences of the Reservation, Hump-ox territory and the lands of the Bison, barren flats and rocky hills stretching for mile upon mile in the lee of the mountains. Windmills pumping water, dry bitten grass and an occasional stand of trees, marked the prefabricated villages where some of the clans still resided. But many of the young were leaving, as Mikklau was leaving, heading for a better life elsewhere.

In the hollow of his stomach he felt a small thrill, a tightening of his nerves that might have been fear or excitement. Excitement, he decided, a wild sense of freedom that almost took away his breath. He had finally done it, finally escaped. There would be no more burying the stinking contents of the lavatory bucket before he breakfasted. No more bullying from Grandmother Cloud. No marrying Rhawna. He could do as he wanted. Go where he wanted. Be answerable to no one but himself.

Yet, underlying his excitement, Mikklau was

aware of the fear – fear of a world that he did not know, a world run by aliens where native people were used for their labour but not really wanted, of towns and cities that were hostile and lonely. James had warned him not to go. J. Samuel Hoddle had warned him. And, dressed as he was, he was likely to get arrested. He glanced at his companion. Sitting at his ease with his back against the end wall of the wagon, swigging whiskey from the bottle, Sam seemed unperturbed about everything.

"What happens if someone finds us in here?" asked Mikklau.

"No chance of that," Sam replied airily.

"But just supposing?"

"We get a thousand dollar fine or sent to jail," said Sam.

Mikklau paled. All he had was the forty-seven dollars fifty clutched in his hand, and James had told him about jail. It was where the aliens confined people who broke their laws. With rapists, murderers and muggers, he could be locked up in a small cell and finally executed.

"Don't look so worried," said Sam. "It's not going to happen. I've been freight-hopping for years and never been caught. Sit down and make yourself comfortable. You want a drink?"

Mikklau shook his head. It was one of Grandmother Cloud's dictates. Alien liquor was forbidden. Nervously, he squatted on his heels as Sam took a final swig and returned the bottle to his pocket.

"Are you a Hump-ox boy or a Bison?" Sam asked him.

"Crowling," murmured Mikklau.

"I didn't know there were Crowlings around Tyler's Bluff."

"We're just a small clan," Mikklau told him.

"So you're off to Kennedy to join your relatives then?"

"What relatives?" asked Mikklau.

"Every large city's got its Crowlings," said Sam. "You'd best go to Gully Town and stay with them, I reckon. I'll see you on the bus tomorrow morning. You hungry, are you?"

Mikklau watched as Sam unbuckled his haversack. On a blue and white chequered napkin spread on the floor he laid out the contents ... pies and pickles, filled bread rolls wrapped in clingfilm, a knife and sponge cake and a bag of apples.

"I like to eat decent," Sam explained. "It's probably not what you're used to, and the rolls are a bit squashed, but I wasn't expecting visitors. This one's smoked salmon, that one's egg mayonnaise, and the pies are chicken tikka. Help yourself."

Mikklau crawled forward. Not caring how it tasted, he wolfed down a share of the food. "You didn't need my money after all!" he said accusingly.

"Call it a deposit on what you're eating," replied Sam.

"Why are you doing this anyway?" asked Mikklau.

"Doing what?" asked Sam.

"Helping me," said Mikklau.

Sam shrugged, nibbled a portion of pie-crust and delicately dabbed his mouth with a soiled handkerchief. "Maybe you remind me of myself," he said. "I wasn't much older than you when I skipped home, and it weren't no picnic. And who taught you table manners, boy?"

"My grandmother," Mikklau informed him.

"Did she never tell you it's impolite to gobble in refined company or speak with your mouth full? Good food is to be lingered over and enjoyed. And go easy on the gherkins or you'll be suffering indigestion later."

Again Sam pulled the whiskey bottle from his pocket, downed another mouthful and carefully wiped its rim before once more offering it to Mikklau. "It's the nearest I've got to vintage wine," he said. "And it's well diluted. Goes further that way, see? I'm not always the complete drunkard I pretend to be."

This time Mikklau accepted, sipped and swallowed, spluttered and coughed and pulled a grimace. It was stronger than the shaman's brew he had drunk the previous night and it tasted equally foul. He gave back the bottle.

"Why do you need to pretend anyway?" he asked.

"It's what people expect," Sam informed him.

"How do you mean?" asked Mikklau.

Sam sliced an apple and pondered. "What I appear to be is just one more drunken bum," he said. "People accept that, see? But if they were to suspect I'm not, then their expectations would change. I wouldn't be able to carry on as I am, unencumbered and travelling the country. And when I hit the cities I wouldn't be able to claim food and clothes and shelter from the local Welfare Department. I'd be expected to knuckle down and become part of the system, get a job and provide for myself, see?"

"I want to get a job," Mikklau confided.

Sam frowned, munched on his apple, and frowned again. "What d'you want a job for, boy? Paid employment's just another form of prostitution. You'll be selling your time and your freedom for a pittance that's barely enough to live on, spending forty odd years of your life doing something you hate. There's too many immigrants now, see? All that's left for your kind is the crap. Washing dishes or emptying garbage, and that's if you're lucky!"

James had said that, Mikklau remembered. But if he was determined enough he was sure to find something.

"I'm not going back to the Reservation!" he said.

"You want to end up like me?" Sam demanded.

In the dim light Mikklau regarded him, a beggar, a vagabond, with untrimmed beard and matted hair, unclean clothes and barley burrs stuck in his hat. Homeless and unkempt, his complexion florid from drink, J. Samuel Hoddle was definitely not the role model Mikklau desired to follow.

Leaning back against the wall, he closed his eyes. The coins were hot in his hand and the midday heat beat like a fist on the roof of the wagon. The inside air was stifling. Effects of food and whiskey fumes, last night's exertion and the rhythm of the wheels along the track, made him feel drowsy. But he knew what kind of future he wanted ... bright as dreams the images flittered through his mind, sprung from the tales Kate Baxter had told him and gleaned from the pages of a glossy magazine he had once seen in the supermarket at Tyler's Bluff – although words to describe it seemed hard to come by and how he would achieve it was another matter.

"There has to be some way," he murmured, but the images fled, were lost among Sam's guffaws of laughter and the sweet sleepy darkness within his own head.

He awoke as the freight-train crossed the Arizona River, disturbed by the rattle of its wheels on the struts of the bridge. It was almost evening. Through the door Sam had opened to let in the air, he saw the sky reflecting in the water, a road bridge in the distance, gnats' wings and shadows. He heard the cry of an unknown bird, sniffed the unfamiliar reek of river weed and oil tankers heading for the open ocean.

"Where are we?" he asked.

He turned his head when Sam failed to answer. With his mouth wide open the vagrant slept and snored. And on the other side of the river the landscape changed. All Mikklau had dreamed of and imagined he saw pass before him – blue lakes in a green countryside and white villas nestling on their shores. There were tall trees, lush vegetation, flowers that lived for more than a moment. He saw smooth lawns and cool fountains, sailing boats on turquoise water, gravel drives and gleaming automobiles. People sipped drinks on patios and kindled barbecues as the evening shadows lengthened.

Excited, Mikklau shook Sam awake.

"That's it," he told him. "That's what I was trying to explain to you ... everything out there!"

The vagrant peered where he pointed.

"That's what I want," said Mikklau.

"Dream on!" muttered Sam.

"Don't you want it, too?" asked Mikklau.

"You serious?" muttered Sam.

"Why shouldn't I be?" asked Mikklau.

Sam coughed and roused himself, spat through the doorway as if he despised what he saw, or else despised Mikklau for wanting it.

"Forget it," he said harshly. "Blue Water District ain't for the likes of us. You got to be rich to buy into a place like that. A billionaire, boy, which is something you and I will never be."

"But most aliens are," said Mikklau. "Outside Tyler's Bluff, that is."

Sam raised an eyebrow. "What cloud-cuckoo-land were you born in, son? Let me tell you, the nearest most of us get to living like that is a take-away pizza on Friday nights and watching it on telly! It's a nice life for the few who have plenty, hard for the rest of us and the bum's rush for indigenous natives. You should have stayed on the Reservation like I told you." Dragging the whiskey bottle from his pocket, he drained its contents and hurled it through the doorway.

Mikklau felt something dying inside him, all he had wanted and hoped for destroyed by Sam's words. An old fear rose in place of it, a fear that there was nothing left for him but a squalor he had yet to know.

"There's got to be something!" he said defiantly.

"You'll find out," muttered Sam.

Darkness fell early, although it was not really dark. A strange dome of light lit the sky, a sickly orange miasma blotting out the moons and stars. Aeroplanes with winking lights sank low towards the far horizon.

Then the city began, its sprawling environs containing gas stations and power stations, factories and housing lots, shopping precincts and leisure centres and drive-in restaurants. It was similar to Tyler's Bluff but on a massive scale, a murmurous noise of people and traffic, a sound in the night like the beating of a giant heart. And the smell of it was stronger than the smell of Sam, or the fading disinfectant smell within the wagon ... smoke and dust and gas-fumes, grease and garbage, and an underlying reek of decay that reminded Mikklau of crowlings.

The freight-train slowed and the single track line became many. Neon signs in a myriad colours advertised goods and services. Lighted commuter trains flashed past and the noise and smells grew stronger, trapped and echoing in the streets between the high-rise blocks.

Mikklau sniffed, and the smell of his new garments struck him. There was a shirt and long-johns warm from wearing and infused with the reek of Sam that wiped out all else. He was to put them on, now, before they left the train, he was instructed. Stripped of a layer of his clothing and swaying to the movement of the wheels across the points, the vagrant buttoned his overcoat, rearranged his woollen hat and scarf, and shouldered his haversack.

"Get a move on!" he commanded. "They ain't the latest fashion but you can't walk down Main Street with nothing on! We'll find you some jeans and a sweatshirt when we get to the hostel."

Revolted, Mikklau obeyed, transferring the forty-seven dollars fifty into the shirt pocket. And the unclean odour became as nothing when the train finally stopped.

They were some way past the main station concourse, up a siding among diesel tanks and wagon sheds, and there were crowlings everywhere. Their droppings cushioned the stones, squelched between Mikklau's toes as he followed Sam back along the track, and the birds themselves scurried from his path in a black stinking tide. More roosted on the roofs and the overhead wires, soda-lights gleaming in millions of tiny malevolent eyes. It was as if they were waiting for something, some kind of signal before they made their attack.

"Mind how you step," whispered Sam.

"There's so many of them!" murmured Mikklau.

"Wherever there's rubbish there are crowlings," muttered Sam. "And there's more rubbish in Kennedy than any other place. The station's central, so they gather here, see? Every morning the Pest Control

Department sprays the area, and every night the danged things are back again."

Small wings fluttered, and the air was filled with their twittering. Droppings from the overhead wires pattered like rain. The stench was inescapable.

"They breed worse than humans!" muttered Sam.

"According to my grandfather, crowlings will survive when all other species become extinct," Mikklau informed him.

"I reckon he could be right," muttered Sam.

"Rubbish should be buried anyway," said Mikklau.

"That a political comment or a racist remark?" asked Sam.

"Pardon?" said Mikklau.

"Nothing," said Sam. "And you want to try telling it to the rest of your kind, boy."

They crossed the main railroad tracks, steel lines shining silver beneath the orange sky, and huddled in an alcove of a graffiti-covered wall as a passenger train rattled past. All around the crowlings rose, fluttered like moths against the lighted windows and crawled through the air vents. Inside a carriage a woman screamed, and Sam started to run, great loping strides towards the main station complex.

"Quick, before they look for a landing place!" shouted Sam.

Mikklau followed. Droppings and bird bodies were crushed beneath his feet, and a few retaliated. Small and vicious, the toothed beaks pecked at his ankles. Others fluttered against his face, tiny claws raking his forehead and the back of his hands as he hurled them away and Sam hauled him onto the nearby platform.

"That was close," muttered the vagrant.

Mikklau wiped away the thin trickles of blood on the sleeve of Sam's shirt and glanced behind. Inexplicably, the birds did not follow. The concourse was clean of their droppings, shops and restaurants open for business, waiting passengers unaware of their presence. It was Mikklau himself people reacted to, or maybe Sam, wrinkling their noses and moving from their path. Others exchanged glances, or pointedly turned their backs as if their nearness was offensive. A space grew around them and Mikklau heard mutterings. Everywhere he looked he saw hard eyes and unfriendly faces, and felt himself hated.

Intimidated, he stayed close to Sam. And for the vagrant, the people on the concourse were a professional challenge. Weaving among them he held out his hand.

"Spare us some change, mister?"

"Two dollars fifty for a cheese sandwich?"

"Money for the boy?"

"A small donation towards food and clothes?"

Their answers were mostly abusive, but one woman opened her purse and gave him a twenty dollar bill. He was to spend it on the child, she instructed. She was looking at Mikklau but he was a man now, not a child, and Sam purchased whiskey in the station supermarket instead, begged his way through the crowded foyer and out into the street.

Mikklau gazed round in confusion. The city centre was ablaze with lights and colours and loud with noise. Traffic and people flowed up and down Main Street between bustling shops and towering buildings. Gas fumes mingled with the scents of burger parlours and hot-dog stands, and flashing signs told him when to walk and when not to.

Gripping his arm, Sam hustled him along, then turned into an empty alley between the shops. It was narrow and ill-lit. A man slept in a doorway. Litter bins over-flowed and the reek of crowlings grew stronger as the darkness increased. Mikklau could sense them roosting in their hundreds on window-sills and overhead gutters, nesting in drains and air-conditioning grilles.

On a street parallel to Main Street, in a converted chapel set among dingy pubs and clubs and striptease joints, was a hostel and soup-kitchen. Still gripping Mikklau's arm, Sam ushered him inside. It was a vast single room with a row of cubicles on one side, tables and chairs on the other, and several closed doors and a lighted serving hatch at the far end. Naked electric light bulbs hung from the ceiling and a few shabby men, dressed similarly to Sam, sat hunched at their separate tables. None looked up when Sam and Mikklau entered, and the clatter of Sam's boots on the floorboards seemed not to disturb the silence.

The vagrant rapped on the service-hatch counter.

"Rooms and board for two, if you please! Preferably en suite. And we'll dine *à la carte*. What's on the menu?"

A girl's face appeared in the space. She had short

hair the colour of straw and wore glasses. Her voice was brusque and efficient. "Shepherd's pie and cabbage with tomato soup for starters. Take a seat and I'll shout to you when it's ready. And we don't provide shelter for juveniles or natives."

"Why's that?" asked Sam.

"Policy," replied the girl. "There's a youth hostel over on Ninth Street, but I wouldn't advise it. He'd be better off going direct to one of the housing camps in Gully Town."

"It's more than ten miles to Gully Town," Sam objected.

"There are buses," said the girl.

"Buses cost money," said Sam.

"Well, he can't stay here. He's under age."

"Where's Pete?" asked Sam.

"He left six months ago," said the girl. "He's working for the Welfare Department in Ohio Town."

"So who's in charge here now?"

"It won't make any difference," said the girl.

"I'll speak with him anyway," Sam said obstinately.

"Eric!" shouted the girl.

A nearby door opened in response.

"Sam!" said Eric. "Long time no see. And who's your friend?"

Officially his name was Mikklau Crowling. He was small in stature as most natives were, dark-haired, purple-eyed and scrawny, no more than a child to alien eyes. A boy among men, and Eric was reluctant to have him stay. But Sam insisted and Mikklau tried

121

to explain. He had become a man the moment he stepped from the train, found his creature and found his adult name. He was no longer Mikklau but he was still Crowling, and he had the scratches to prove it.

"See?" said Sam.

"He can't be more than thirteen at most!" objected the girl.

"He's adult in native terms," Sam insisted.

"He can stay for tonight," agreed Eric. "But no longer."

"Tonight's all we're asking," said Sam.

"And make sure he bolts his door."

Later, fed and showered and duly accommodated, Mikklau lay alone in the cubicle next to Sam. Clothes, selected from a back room full of donations, were folded on the end of his bed ready for the morning: a pair of worn jeans and a tee-shirt, socks and underpants and a pair of shabby sneakers. Orange light shone through the open window, traffic roared in the distance and, even above the odours of cooking and vagrants, Mikklau could smell crowlings. It was as if they were part of the place, enmeshed in the fabric of the city, lurking behind the glittering life of it like an underlying essence of decay.

His first thrill at escaping from the Reservation was dulled by the reality in which he found himself. Nothing in Kennedy was as he imagined it to be and nothing had happened the way he planned it, although maybe tomorrow when Sam took him to Gully Town things would be different. Maybe, among the native people, he would feel welcomed. And if his dreams for the future were somewhat diminished they were not entirely dead. He would settle for an ordinary house in an ordinary suburb, he decided, a washing machine and a television and a pick-up truck. All else he had seen in Blue Water District and the glossy magazine were trappings he could do without.

The clothes made Mikklau feel alien. Socks and sneakers cushioned his feet and, when he walked, the legs of his jeans rubbed together with a soft swish of sound. Except for the length and darkness of his hair and the colour of his eyes, there was nothing left to remind him of the person he had been. Even the smell of his own body had been washed away, replaced by carbolic soap and fabric conditioner. The person who left the hostel with Sam in the morning was a comparative stranger.

Double doors closed and were bolted behind them. The outside air reeked of pesticides and disinfectant, and the drab street was silent in the bright early sunlight, its buildings on one side stark with shadows. Sidewalks were wet and shining, window sills washed clean of droppings. The only bad smell was Sam, thought Mikklau, although he sensed that somewhere the birds remained. He heard the whistle of a diesel locomotive in the Central Station, the distant rattle of a tram car and the yelp of a dog along the alley. And did he imagine, at the corners of his vision, a tiny flutter of wings?

The dog was dead by the time they reached it and

almost indistinguishable, a horde of crowlings feasting on its carcass. Sickened, Mikklau paused and stared.

"It was alive just now," he said. "I heard it yelp."

"More'n likely," muttered Sam.

"So they must have killed it," said Mikklau.

"Better a dog than a person," muttered Sam.

"But they don't do that," said Mikklau.

"Don't do what?" asked Sam.

"Kill," said Mikklau. "Unless it was dying anyway."

Sam shrugged, shambled on and turned into Main Street. It looked different by day, grey and colourless, its glittering shops not yet open for business. The burger stalls were locked. Yesterday's litter drifted in the breeze. Native men wearing navy-blue coveralls gathered it into bags, and a road-sweeping machine sucked dust and dead crowlings from the gutters.

"Where are we going?" asked Mikklau.

"*You*'re going to Gully Town," said Sam.

"What about you?" asked Mikklau.

"What about me?" asked Sam.

"Aren't you coming with me?"

"I reckon I've babysat you long enough," said Sam.

"But I don't know where Gully Town is!" said Mikklau.

"I'll put you on the bus," promised Sam.

Then Mikklau would truly be alone. The fear gripped him, churned in his stomach with the hostel breakfast of eggs and beans. He had known Sam for barely a day but he could not imagine being without him. With his beard and whiskey bottle, body odour and unclean clothes, the vagrant protected him, kept people at bay.

It was people Mikklau was afraid of. Not the quiet native women who cleaned the shops and offices and were now heading homewards, but the alien people with their pale faces and strange coloured eyes. A sudden influx came hurrying from the train station and there were more in the bus terminus. Men carrying briefcases, girls wearing tight skirts and high-heeled shoes, older women clutching handbags and spotty executive youths, went scurrying away towards the banks and business centres, shopping arcades or high-rise office blocks. And when they had gone, more arrived, hundreds, maybe thousands, on every bus that pulled in.

As Sam studied the route schedules, Mikklau noticed the expressions of those who noticed him, looks of distaste or disdain or, occasionally, pity. But no one spoke or approached. Whatever they felt about him was nothing compared to what they felt about Sam. One glance at the vagrant, one glimpse of the whiskey bottle in his pocket, triggered a fear mixed with loathing that drove all but the uniformed staff away.

"Move along, sir!" said the security guard. "And you," he said to Mikklau. "We have laws against loitering in this city."

"Who's loitering?" asked Sam.

"I've been watching you these last ten minutes!"

"Where's the route schedule for Gully Town?" Sam demanded.

"Buses for Gully Town leave from Lugg Street," replied the man.

Muttering, Sam departed and Mikklau followed, back along Main Street the way they had come. The street-cleaning gang had departed and the buildings absorbed the crowds of commuters. Rush-hour traffic filled the air with gas fumes and noise. Shuttered shops opened for trade, Kennedy's rich façade that displayed a lifestyle Mikklau could not share. Price tags in the windows depressed him, placed everything he saw beyond his reach, and however much he earned he realised it would never be enough.

"Five hundred dollars for a denim jacket?" he said.

"It don't pay to window-shop," said Sam.

They took to the back streets, walked through an area of taverns, seedy apartments and makeshift workshops. Paint peeled from doors and windows. Weeds grew through the cracks in the sidewalk, and the roadside gutters were choked with litter. This was the kind of area he would live in, Mikklau supposed, although he sensed no native presence, just an atmosphere of menace that had nothing to do with crowlings. Alien eyes watched from dark interiors. Pale-faced men in grease-stained coveralls on a garage forecourt noted his passing, and a group of youths outside a pool hall barred his way.

Sam gripped his arm and ushered him across the street. And the youths followed, eight of them in all,

with shaven heads and hard faces. Mikklau did not
hear what they shouted. Their words were lost in an
upsurge of fear, and the sound of his own heart
hammering as Sam quickened his pace.

"Move!" hissed the vagrant.

"What do they want with us?" asked Mikklau.

"It ain't no good whatever it is," muttered Sam.

The jeers increased. Flung stones rattled in their
wake, and a woman standing in a doorway watched
and laughed. Sam's shambling steps lengthened to a
run, taking Mikklau with him. His breathing was
harsh and his great-coat flapped around his legs.
Sweat on his forehead glistened in the sun as he
rounded the corner.

Voices echoed behind them along an alley.

"Clear off, you stinking aborigine!"

"We don't want your kind here!"

"What jobs are left are ours!"

"They mean me!" said Mikklau.

"Just keep moving!" puffed Sam.

They entered a different street, a grimy
thoroughfare flanked by cheap shops and thronged
with traffic and people. Native men and women
squatted on the sidewalks among an array of
artefacts – painted gourds, pots and baskets and
bright woven shawls. Bare-footed children sold luck-
stones or begged for money. Between the buildings,
Mikklau could glimpse the docks by the harbour and
factory chimneys beyond. Tram-rails shone silver
along the centre of the street, and orange buses idled
at the roadside.

Hauled aboard a bus for Gully Town North and forced to pay the fare for both himself and Sam, Mikklau was unsure if the group of youths had followed him or not. All he felt was relief when the door sighed shut, and concern for Sam when he joined him in the long back seat. Legs outstretched, coat and shirt unbuttoned, his face coloured red as the desert sands at sunset and heaving for breath, the vagrant was accompanying him after all, although he was barely aware of it. Taking off his woollen hat, Sam mopped the sweat from his face.

"I need a drink," he wheezed.

Mikklau unscrewed the whiskey bottle, placed it in Sam's shaking hand, and in the mirror the driver watched. A single swallow was all Sam had before the bus stopped. "There's no alcohol allowed on this vehicle!" shouted the driver. "If you want to drink, squire, then you get off! Right now!" Half a dozen passengers turned their heads as J. Samuel Hoddle rose cumbersomely from his seat.

Mikklau clutched his arm.

"Please don't go!" he begged.

Something communicated ... a need, perhaps, or a desperation, an unspoken fear of being on his own ... something Sam heard and heeded and instinctively understood. Pocketing the bottle, he nodded to the driver and sat back down. He was still breathing heavily as the bus pulled off again.

"Blooming rules and regulations!" muttered Sam. "Walk. Don't walk. No alcohol. No spitting. I can't be doing with it, see? If I wasn't so bushed I'd have told him where to go! And now you know the benefits of freight-hopping, boy. There ain't no rules when you're freight-hopping, or hitching, or travelling by shanks's pony. But buy a blooming ticket and you can't even fart without someone's say-so. Are you hearing me?"

"Yes," Mikklau said meekly.

"So mind you remember it," said Sam.

Sunlight sweltered through the dusty windows, and he closed his eyes, a middle-aged vagrant growing old before his time. The philosophy he preached was of no use to Mikklau nor was his life-style what Mikklau wished to pursue, but there was something between them, some kind of mutual caring. He watched as Sam's breathing eased and his colour returned to normal. Then, reassured, he turned his attention to the scenery passing outside.

Passengers boarded and alighted as the bus headed north and west. Docks and factories gave way to residential housing lots. It was not like the Blue Water District, but it would do, thought Mikklau. He would not object to living in one of those clapboard bungalows with a shady front porch, a tree outside and a small area of lawn. He touched Sam's arm.

"Is it all right to want that?" he asked.

The vagrant squinted through the window.

"Just wake me when we get to Gully Town," he said.

During the ride Mikklau's hopes lifted. There were obviously jobs to be had. He saw native men emptying garbage bins in a shady cul-de-sac, others hacking up the road for a cable television company. More worked on out-of-town construction sites, mixing concrete or carrying bricks. Others, on a newly-designated business park, erected the metal frameworks of workshops and warehouses, and there were hundreds working on the new Kennedy ring-road. Stripped to the waist, their dusky torsos gleaming in the sun, they laboured with picks and shovels among acres of raw earth, rode on or drove the great yellow machines. Alien overseers wearing hard hats strode among them.

Beyond the ring-road the city ended. Nothing remained but tumbled hills and miles of dereliction, flooded stone quarries, clay pits and gravel pits, spoil heaps and landfill sites. And there was no one left on the bus but Sam and Mikklau – and a growing stench that belonged to neither. Soon, where the hard road ended at the gates of an abandoned cement works, the bus stopped and the driver switched off the engine. Sam snored softly in the sudden silence and Mikklau nudged him.

"We must be there," he said uncertainly.

"Where?" muttered Sam.

"Gully Town," said Mikklau.

"Hurry up, you two!" shouted the driver. "We don't go any further!"

"You carry on," Sam told Mikklau.

Mikklau understood. This was as far as Sam would go and he was on his own now. There was no appeal and no goodbyes, nothing left to say. With his woollen hat pulled down over his eyes, the vagrant had already settled back to sleep. Reluctant without him, Mikklau rose to leave.

"*And* your companion!" shouted the driver. "I want you both off! I've a half-hour coffee break here and no one gets on board for the return journey until I say so."

"For Christ's sake!" shouted Sam. "Can't a body be left in peace? A quiet kip in the back seat ain't much to ask!"

"Not on my bus!" replied the driver.

Grabbing his haversack, Sam lurched to his feet and followed Mikklau down the aisle. The doors sighed open before them and the stench increased, a waft of heat-laden air thick with the smells of garbage and excrement and crowlings.

"I'll be back in twenty-five minutes," vowed Sam.

"Don't you ever wash?" asked the driver.

The doors rattled shut before Sam could reply, and Mikklau saw no trace of Gully Town. On past the cement factory the road became a rutted track that led through the scarred land towards the sky, or else ended at a sheer edge some distance ahead. White water lay pooled in the ruts, splashed beneath Sam's boots as he shambled along it. Mikklau's sneakers were covered in pale mud.

"How do you know this is the way?" he asked.

"By following my nose!" the vagrant said crossly.

They came upon it suddenly. The track angled down the steep side of a gorge, and they were standing near the head of it where the sides came together and a small stream tumbled over a rim of rock. But the sound of falling water was drowned by the din from beneath them ... human voices ... men, women and children ... thousands upon thousands of native people all crammed together in a sprawling shanty town of tin shacks and wooden sheds and polythene dwellings.

"There's your Gully Town," said Sam.

There, too, was the source of the smell. Mikklau stared, appalled by what he saw. They had forgotten who they were, forgotten how to live cleanly. Rubbish piles heaved with crowlings, and instead of streets were terraced walkways of sewage and mud. On the opposite slope was a recent landfill site. A fleet of yellow machines bulldozed the city refuse over the edge and the people sorted through it, people and crowlings tearing open the polythene sacks for anything that might be of use. It was how they clothed themselves, fed themselves, fuelled their cooking fires and furnished their shelters. They were scavengers, all of them, along with the birds who dwelt among them and whose name they shared.

"Crowlings," muttered Sam. "Same as you, see?"

"No!" said Mikklau.

"Better to live with your own kind than live with us."

"No!" repeated Mikklau.

"There's a welfare kitchen somewhere, on down the valley, so you won't starve," said Sam. "And works buses come every morning to pick up labourers. You might be lucky. You never know."

"I don't want to live like that!" cried Mikklau.

"Well, there ain't nothing else," Sam said reasonably. "It's the same on the outskirts of every big city. You'll get used to it, I reckon. And it's bound to improve, given time." His heavy hand rested briefly on Mikklau's shoulder. "Off you go," he urged.

It was the nearest Sam came to saying goodbye. Turning in his tracks and dragging the whiskey bottle from his pocket, he went ambling back towards the parked bus, leaving Mikklau alone with the vision of his future, the squalor his own race had created.

It was a kind of death that Mikklau faced, the death of his dreams, the death of hope. Gully Town stank of it, a living death for all who resided there. The tin roofs rusted. The wooden shacks rotted. Crowlings feasted on the unburied faeces and bred in the garbage dumps, thrived where native people sickened. Mikklau thought he could not bear to go down there, yet he had no choice.

His feet skidded in the soft mud as he headed down the track, and the stench increased. A native woman with leg ulcers and an empty shopping bag, intent on catching the bus, hurried past him, a group of youths came trailing behind her. They reminded Mikklau of the other group of youths he and Sam had run from, except that they were native and clad in nothing but shorts. Their black hair was matted and unkempt, and their purple eyes gazed into his without empathy or liking before shifting to his clothes, noting the comparative cleanliness of his shirt and jeans and sneakers. Then, leering and aggressive, they barred Mikklau's way.

"What do you want?" he asked fearfully.

"Whatever you've got," one of them replied.

Mikklau stepped to one side, tried to dodge them, kicked and shouted as they grabbed him. An arm fastened around his throat. Hands grabbed his legs, felt in his pockets and relieved him of his money. They would have stripped him of his jeans and sneakers, too, but the woman with leg ulcers had turned at his cry. Brandishing her shopping bag and shouting at the top of her voice, she headed back down the path towards him. And the youths ran off, returned to the cesspit that was Gully Town, leaving Mikklau lying on his back in the mud.

The woman bent over him.

"You all right, boy?"

"They robbed me!" moaned Mikklau.

"It could have been worse," said the woman. She put down her shopping bag. Skinny fingers helped haul him to his feet. "You're new here, aren't you?"

"Yes," admitted Mikklau.

"Best return where you came from," the woman advised.

She left him then, toiled back up the gully, not waiting to see what he did. He was penniless now, stuck where he was, alone and desperate with no one to help him, unable even to pay the bus fare back to Kennedy. Unless he could catch up with Sam? He made up his mind. Following the woman, Mikklau ran, willing to beg for the rest of his life if he had to.

Robbed by his own kind, his clothes ruined, Mikklau

returned to Kennedy on the same bus that had brought him to Gully Town and, this time, Sam paid the fare. He had not had to beg. The vagrant accepted that he refused to live there and, apart from begrudging the small capital outlay required for his return transportation, there were no other recriminations. And there was a man Sam knew living up north who might give Mikklau a job.

Mikklau's eyes shone. "You mean a real job?"

"Maybe," said Sam.

"Why didn't you say so before?"

"I only just thought of it," said Sam. "And I'm making no promises, neither."

It was all Mikklau could get out of him. He would not say what the job was nor where exactly, just somewhere up north, a two-day journey by rail. But it was something to hope for, something to plan for. And even if they travelled by freight they were going to need to purchase supplies, said Mikklau, food and whiskey and water.

"How will we do that without money?" he asked.

"I'm not without resources," said Sam.

"What resources?"

In answer Sam touched his nose, pulled the woollen hat over his eyes, and once more settled to sleep.

It was midday in Lugg Street when they alighted, and Mikklau brushed the dried mud of Gully Town from his jeans. The day's heat had built up and the sky was growing dark. The city seemed airless. Sheet lightning flickered beyond the docks. Goods, previously displayed on the sidewalks, had been taken inside and native traders were packing up their unsold artefacts. Shoppers boarded trams and buses, or otherwise scurried away, and Lugg Street emptied as they walked along it.

"Why is everyone leaving?" asked Mikklau.

"There's going to be a storm," muttered Sam.

A thunder clap, louder than the noise of traffic, rolled overhead and rain began to fall in warm heavy drops. Sam took shelter in a doorway, but Mikklau laughed, held out his hands and raised his face to the sky. He had never known rain such as this before, never experienced it, great grey sheets of it sluicing from the clouds. He was soaked in seconds. Traffic stopped and the streets were awash. Sidewalks shone with reflected light from the shops.

"You get out of it, boy!" Sam said wrathfully.

"You too, mate!" said the shopkeeper from behind him. "I don't want no vagrants hanging about in my doorway! It's off-putting to customers!"

Head bent and muttering, his shoulders hunched and his hands thrust deep in his pockets, Sam shuffled on along the street with Mikklau dancing beside him. They lingered, briefly, in an arcade of pinball machines but, yet again, Sam was moved on. Through quiet back streets and empty alleys where the water leaked from overhead gutters and runnelled down the drains, they walked together. Rain darkened the back of Sam's greatcoat and finally, as Mikklau began to feel cold, they entered the Welfare Offices on Eighth Avenue.

Alien staff behind glass-fronted counters eyed them warily ... a native boy in mud-soiled clothes and a middle-aged vagrant. Rain dripped from Sam's hair and beard, made grimy pools on the pale linoleum floor, and Mikklau's sneakers squelched as he walked.

"Take a seat, please."

There were no other clients. Under the striplights on a row of hard chairs they sat and waited until, eventually, they were called to one of the counters. Being a native, Mikklau was not entitled to a Welfare allowance, but Sam could claim twelve dollars a day for food and essentials. There were forms to fill in, another wait while they were processed, and yet another wait in another office before Sam was given the cash.

By then the rain had stopped. Wet streets steamed in the sunlight and, just for an hour or so, the city smelled sweet as if the air itself had been washed clean. Sam bought whiskey from an off-licence with the Welfare money, sat on a polythene bag on the cathedral steps until the bottle was half empty and Mikklau's clothes were dry, then begged outside the train station during the afternoon rush hour. Heat and dust and noise and hunger, the smells of traffic fumes and crowlings, made Mikklau feel queasy, and all Sam gained was two dollars fifty.

"Stingy blooming lot!" the vagrant muttered.

Mikklau did not like to ask, but in the end he had to. "I'm hungry, Sam. I've had nothing to eat since breakfast and nor have you. And where will we find food for the journey?"

"I told you," said Sam. "I'm not without resources."

"You spent it on whiskey!" Mikklau reminded him.

"That was a bonus," said Sam.

Daylight was fading and the orange darkness had begun to deepen when, with the last of the commuters, Sam and Mikklau re-entered the station foyer. Security guards watched and Mikklau stared as Sam fed a banker's card into the cashpoint machine and extracted a hundred dollars. He was not ungenerous. He bought Mikklau an anorak from a clothes store on the station concourse. It was a deep blue waterproof with a quilted lining and fake fur around the hood. It smelled of newness and reached almost to his knees. He would need it, said Sam. It was cold up north.

Mikklau carried it proudly, neatly folded in a large plastic shopper, an alien possession he had never thought to own. It made him feel closer to the people around him, almost as if he were one of them. He was a traveller on the concourse ... a shopper in the supermarket where Sam filled his haversack with fruit and pies and sandwiches, canned sardines and bottled water ... a diner in a self-service café waiting at a table with the bag on the floor beside him as Sam loaded a tray with fries and burgers. But his sense of belonging did not last.

Vagrants were unwelcome in Kennedy City and unwelcome in that restaurant. And so, too, was

Mikklau. The woman at the cash desk refused to take Sam's money. And when Sam complained, she called the manageress who ordered both of them to eat at the outside tables.

"And don't take all night!" she warned.

"We ain't flaming started yet!" grumbled Sam.

People stared at them through the café windows and several customers seated nearby promptly moved away. The new blue anorak in its plastic shopping bag had changed nothing. There was nothing Mikklau could do to disguise his origins, the long hair, dusky skin and purple eyes that marked him as a native. But Sam had a choice. He did not have to be what he was. He could wash and shave and change his clothes, be like everyone else, instead of deliberately alienating himself from his own kind. He was not penniless either and he had no need to beg. Mikklau wondered why he did it, and who J. Samuel Hoddle really was.

"Eat up!" Sam told him. "It's the last hot meal you'll be having for a while. And there ain't nothing worse than luke-warm fries."

"Everyone hates us, don't they?" Mikklau said miserably.

"What if they do?" said Sam. "It's their problem, boy, and it don't do to mind what people think of you."

The longed-for burger was a disappointment, the bun soggy and the meat tasteless as rubber, the fries almost cold and limp with grease. And the noise and movement was a constant distraction. A sweeping machine drove to and fro. Long-distance trains arrived and departed. A voice over the tannoy system announced times and destinations, and people carrying suitcases went scurrying towards the various platforms. Computer screens flickered. And the two railroad security guards patrolled past their table at regular intervals, intent on moving them on the moment they had finished eating. Sam leant forward.

"Don't rush it," he whispered.

"I couldn't if I wanted to," said Mikklau.

"Not to your liking?" asked Sam. "If you want to live as we do, boy, you'll have to get used to badly cooked junk food. There won't be much else where you're going."

"Where *am* I going?" asked Mikklau.

"North," Sam repeated.

"But where exactly?"

"Half a dozen miles past Jasper's Creek," said Sam. "Out on the North-South Highway. A place called Lou and Percy's diner ... although there ain't no Lou any more. She died of cancer a few years ago. Only forty-two, she was. But last time I was there Percy was looking for someone."

"You mean he's the man who might give me a job?" asked Mikklau.

"It's worth a try," said Sam. "And we got to time things proper, slip past them security guards, see? You be ready when I tell you, right?"

Mikklau poked at the French fries still on his plate as, yet again, the railroad security guards strolled towards them. He had heard of Jasper's Creek. It was where the star-people had held Grandfather Crowling and Grandmother Cloud on their journey south, the most awful place in the world. But no place could be worse than Gully Town, thought Mikklau, although if Percy was anything like Sam he could not be sure. But he had no time to question or change his mind. When the railroad security guards had passed, Sam shouldered his haversack and heaved himself to his feet.

"Now!" he hissed.

Mikklau picked up the carrier containing his anorak and they both slipped away, hurrying with a crowd of other passengers along a lighted platform beside a long-distance train to the Southern Gulf that was currently being boarded. At the far end where the lights grew dim, the locomotive roared and the platform sloped downward to give access to the open track, they might have been spotted. Warning signs told them that no passengers were allowed beyond that point. But Sam shambled on regardless and their luck held.

They were simply shadows in the orange darkness. They crossed the wide expanse of shining silver rails and headed up a siding, and again no one saw them. Among fuel tanks and wagon sheds where crowlings roosted on every available roof and ledge, and the stench of their droppings made Sam smell wholesome, they settled to wait for the next empty freight-train going north.

On the second day of their journey the weather became noticeably colder. It was not the crisp clear coldness of the desert that Mikklau was used to, but an insidious cold that slowly numbed his feet and fingers and chilled him to the bone. The wind, whistling through the slats of the wagon, made an ache in his face as he watched the landscape passing. Trees were leafless, the afternoon sunless. Darkness fell early and hoarfrost whitened the landscape at the onset of night.

Food at supper tasted frozen. Cold pies, cold sandwiches, added to the overall chill, although Sam seemed not to notice. Hunched in his great-coat, with his hands thrust beneath his armpits and his woollen hat pulled down over his ears, he dozed away the time. But even wearing the new anorak Mikklau was too cold to sleep. The only source of warmth was Sam himself, the vagrant's body-heat slowly seeping into him as, heedless of the smell, Mikklau nestled against him.

When he awoke there was snow on the prairies, an unbroken whiteness stretching away to the far horizon, its coldness reflected by the colourless sky. Except on the peaks of the South Sierras, Mikklau had never seen snow before. His breath made smoke and his teeth chattered. He had to stamp on the floor of the wagon and blow into his cupped hands to restore the circulation to his feet and fingers.

"Must you make so much racket?" muttered Sam.

"I'm cold," said Mikklau.

"You need more clothes, boy."

"Like a bearskin mantle," said Mikklau.

"The fur trade's been banned," Sam informed him.

"My grandmother has one," said Mikklau.

"There ain't no bears in the desert," said Sam.

"My grandparents brought bear pelts with them," explained Mikklau. "Before we were Crowlings we were Luppa, the Wolf-clan. We lived in the northern forests at the foot of a mountain by a lake shaped like an arrow."

"I've heard of Lake Arrow," said Sam.

"We were cleared," said Mikklau. "Over fifty years ago now."

"To make way for ski-slopes," muttered Sam.

"What are ski-slopes?" asked Mikklau.

"A winter playground for rich folks," said Sam.

It was winter now in the land outside although, according to Sam, they had missed the worst of it. Northern winters were long, said Sam, months of snow and bitter cold, and it would probably last for a few weeks yet. And despite the tales Grandfather Crowling had told of a log-house in the forest and the great central hearth where a wood fire burned throughout the days and nights, Mikklau could not imagine how any living thing could survive the reality. It was surprising what did, said Sam. And it was not the weather that destroyed the wolf and the ice-bear and the great bakkau lizard, that raided the nests of fire-eagles or shot them from the sky.

"It seems whatever gets in our way has to go," Sam said bitterly. "Be it bird, beast or native, there ain't no room for anything on this planet apart from us. Given a choice between a motorway or some creature's habitat, we goes for the motorway every time. But I'll not be a party to it, see?"

Mikklau stared at him. The things he said were similar to the things old Joel Baxter had said, and his voice contained the same anger, but his reaction was different.

"Is that why you became a vagrant?" asked Mikklau.

"Among other reasons," said Sam. He took a large swig and replaced the cap. "How about you?" he said. "Tyler's Bluff ain't Gully Town, so what are you running from? Ain't you got a family there who cares for you?

Mikklau shrugged. It was not lack of caring that drove him away. Skooa and his grandparents had always cared. It was the restrictions their caring placed on him that he could not accept. They bound him to the past, to outmoded traditions and beliefs, to a way of life that was totally stagnant, that allowed for no changes, no progression, no improvement. As it was now with them, so it would always be.

"And that's not what I want," said Mikklau.

"Our ways ain't no better," Sam said sourly.

"But I don't know that," said Mikklau.

"It's a rat-race, boy! Believe you me!"

"That's what James said, and I'm not saying you and he are wrong. I just need a chance to find out."

"So what about *them*?" asked Sam.

"Who?" asked Mikklau.

"Your folks," said Sam. "While you're finding out

144

they're going to be worrying what's become of you."

"I'm not a child any more," said Mikklau.

"What's that got to do with it?" asked Sam. "You could be dead, for all they know! And if you're alive they need to know where you are."

But not yet, thought Mikklau, not while he was homeless and penniless and had no prospects, while he was travelling with a vagrant and worse off than he had ever been on the Reservation. He did not want anyone to know that ... not his father, nor his grandparents, nor James Baxter. He would wait until he got where he was going, to Lou and Percy's diner, where maybe Percy would offer him a job. Or maybe he would wait until he had something to show for himself, until he had saved his wages and bought a clapboard bungalow and a pick-up truck.

"I'll tell them one day," he promised.

"When pigs grow wings!" muttered Sam.

The train arrived in Jasper's Creek early in the afternoon, pulling into a siding behind the cattle market. They had to wait until it was safe to disembark, Sam had said. Until a gang of railroad workers wearing garish orange coveralls had checked the couplings of another stationary freight-train, and others in the distance cleared snow from the points.

They waited for hours. Sam dozed in his great-coat and Mikklau kept watch until the railroad workers packed up their tools and headed for home. Only then did Sam shoulder his haversack and agree to leave.

The cold was intense. Snow cracked beneath

Mikklau's sneakers, chilling his feet as they crossed the sidings. Through a tear in the wire of a perimeter fence, they gained access to wasteland beside the cattle market, picked their way across concrete foundations of demolished workshops, piles of loose bricks and thorn-briars covered in snow. Billboards along the roadside advertised it for sale as a reclamation site, and passing traffic sprayed salted slush on their legs as they headed for the town centre.

Mikklau remembered that when Grandfather Ben and Grandmother Cloud were here, Jasper's Creek was still being built. Now, just two generations later, large tracts of it were being demolished. Joel Baxter had told him that the ancient ruined cities that were scattered across the planet had survived for millennia, and even Grandmother Cloud's marriage tent was still intact, but it seemed that nothing the star-people made was intended to last – including Mikklau's anorak. Warm from walking he tried to undo it, and the zip jammed and broke.

"That's how it works," Sam informed him.

"How what works?" asked Mikklau.

"Everything," said Sam.

"I don't understand," said Mikklau.

"Consumerism," said Sam. "The buy-it-and-break-it, or get-fed-up-with-it-and-throw-it-away syndrome. You think about it, boy. The people who make things will never be out of a job and you'll have to slave for the rest of your days to keep replacing what you have. That what you want, is it?"

"You know what I want," Mikklau said stubbornly.

"I know what you think you want," muttered Sam. "A job, a clapboard bungalow and a pick-up truck. Not forgetting the fitted carpets, the telly and the washing machine and the backyard lounger. What's wrong with what you had at the Reservation?"

"It wasn't mine!" said Mikklau.

"Whose was it then?" asked Sam.

"Theirs!" said Mikklau. "*They* made the adobe bricks and built the house ... my father, my grandfather, the rest of the clan! And Grandmother Cloud chose Rhawna to be my wife! I don't want it and I don't want her! I want to make my own way! Right?"

"Lucky you met me then," Sam replied.

Mikklau frowned at the hunched figure before him, shambling along the frozen sidewalk beneath the orange lights. Televisions flickered behind the closed curtains of neat residential homes. Cars gleamed in the driveways. Trees in the gardens were festooned with icicles, and snow on the roofs had melted from the centrally-heated warmth. Luck, thought Mikklau, would have granted him one of those and provided him with a less odorous, more generally acceptable travelling companion than a vagrant. A woman walking a dog crossed the street to avoid them. Police in a patrol car stopped to question their intentions, and the proprietor of a café in the out-of-town shopping precinct bolted the door as they approached. And, once on the freeway where

Sam started hitching, car drivers and truck drivers refused to give them a ride.

Flurries of fresh snow, the wind from the north blowing in their faces, a broken zipper on his anorak and a ten-mile walk to Lou and Percy's diner ... that was Mikklau's kind of luck. The orange glow of the town faded behind him and the darkness deepened. Snow mounds were piled alongside the wet, ghostly shine of the road and the headlights of the oncoming traffic blinded him. His feet and legs were soaked with spray.

"How much further?"

"We walk until we arrive," Sam said helpfully.

It was a long, cold, miserable walk over miles and hours, where the wind bit through the gap in Mikklau's anorak, and snow dripped from the sodden fur of his hood, and Sam tramped before him at a never-changing pace. Here and there, across the distances, small lights shone in remote farmsteads, but they grew fewer as the night grew later, and the flow of traffic eased and almost ceased. Only the occasional truck going north or south, and the shuffle of Sam's boots along the roadway, disturbed the vast windswept silence of the land.

It was the silence that urged Mikklau on, or something within it. He had begun to believe he would never reach where they were going, that he would die in the snow at the side of the road and never be found, but the silence drew him, touched him deep within his soul. A scent on the wind of something strange, yet familiar, far away in the darkness ahead, compelled him to continue. His feet were so cold he could not feel them, and each step was an effort, but there was a thrill of excitement inside him and he needed to find the source of it, know what it was. Heedless of the wind and darkness, of the neon lights among a stand of fir trees, he kept on walking.

Finally Sam called to him. "Oy! Mikklau! Where you off to?"

Mikklau stopped and turned round. The vagrant was standing on the edge of a parking lot where several articulated trucks had pulled in. Beyond was a long, low building huddled among the trees. Mikklau could not read the lighted letters but he guessed it must be Lou and Percy's diner. He could see a coffee machine behind the counter and a crowd of burly men sitting at tables in a curtainless room.

"We're here," said Sam. "Ain't you coming in?"

Just for a moment Mikklau hesitated.

"There ain't nothing on along the road but Halifax City," Sam assured him. "And that's a hundred and fifty miles further north."

Whatever Mikklau had sensed in the darkness ahead had not been Halifax City and the faint, elusive scent on the wind faded when someone opened the diner door. What beckoned him then were the smells of coffee and cooking and the warmth of a log-burning stove, the needs of his body stronger than the calling of his soul.

Inside was a bliss of heat and light, a grimy room with stark cream walls, furnished with red vinyl chairs and tables, the air thick with steam and smoke and quiet conversation. Grease fumes rose from the fryer, the coffee machine hissed and spat, and no one stared at them, objected to them being there or departed in protest. The fat, red-faced proprietor, cooking eggs and bacon on the griddle, barely gave them a second glance.

"Take a seat. I'll be with you in a minute," he said.

"Evening, Percy," said Sam.

The proprietor flipped the egg and glanced towards him, a bearded vagrant with snow melting on his hat and beading his whiskers. Pleased recognition dawned in Percy's eyes. "Well, I'll be jiggered! If it isn't J. Samuel Hoddle himself! Talk of the devil! Sam, you old son-of-a-gun! Where've you been these last two years?"

"Still managing on your own?" asked Sam.

"As usual," said Percy. "They come and go and no one stays for long."

"It's the isolation," said Sam.

"I reckon," said Percy.

Sam placed a hand on Mikklau's shoulder. "Here's one who's willing," he said.

Percy glanced at him, a brief appraising look, noting his youth and his nativeness, the slightness of his build. Then, frowning to himself and saying nothing, he turned back to his griddle, slid the eggs and bacon onto a warmed plate, added beans and sausage and proceeded to load a tray.

"Have a seat," he repeated.

"He won't give you no trouble," said Sam.

Percy picked up the laden tray. "We'll talk about it later," he said.

At eleven o'clock, when the last customer had left, Percy closed the doors and pulled down the blinds, switched off the fryer and the coffee machine, loaded the dishwasher and dimmed the lights. He lived in rooms behind the restaurant, a bedroom and sitting-room originally intended for staff, but Mikklau was not invited. It was not a snub exactly, Percy was far too genial and patronly for that, but Sam was family and had the sofa and Mikklau had a sleeping bag on the floor in front of the stove.

"It'll do for tonight," said Percy.

Warm and well fed, with a cushion beneath his head, Mikklau lay quiescent as Percy turned off the light and retired to his quarters. One night, Mikklau supposed, was something to be grateful for. The dishwasher rattled through its programme and, alone in the neon darkness, he heard a chink of whiskey glasses in the small back sitting-room, caught snatches of conversation through the partly open door.

"He'll be useful to you," Sam insisted.

"Never mind him," said Percy. "What about you? Isn't it time you gave up the road and settled down?"

"You mean here?" said Sam.

"You're a trained chef," said Percy.

"It don't take a chef to cook what you turn out here," said Sam.

"Lou always hoped—" said Percy.

"Lou ain't around no more!"

"You're not getting any younger," said Percy. "And

151

we can't grieve for ever. You told me at the time that life goes on—"

"Is that why you're dossing in these rooms?"

"It's handier living on the actual premises."

"Don't give me that!" said Sam. "The bungalow's only a minute's walk across the parking lot!"

"You don't know what it's like living there without Lou!"

"She *was* my sister," said Sam.

The dishwasher hissed.

"So what's your objection?" asked Sam.

"It's nothing personal," said Percy.

"But rather a bum than a native?" guessed Sam.

"He's just a boy!" said Percy. "I'm running a business, not a children's charity!"

"He can work as well as the next!" said Sam.

"The answer's still no," said Percy.

"That ain't what Lou would have said," muttered Sam.

Crockery in the dishwasher clattered, and a log slipped on the fire. Mikklau rolled over and pulled the sleeping bag up round his ears. Sam could talk all night and it would make no difference. Percy would never agree to employ him. A feeling of dull despair settled in his stomach. Nothing remained but to go home to the Reservation or else stay on the road with Sam. And, whichever alternative he chose, he would achieve nothing.

He awoke, suddenly, when Percy raised the blinds. He crawled from his sleeping bag and pulled on his sneakers. Early morning sunlight dazzled his eyes and the diner looked even dingier than it had the previous night, its walls streaked with grease, its brown linoleum soiled with mud and food scraps, the red vinyl tables and chairs stained and scratched and in need of wiping. The air smelt stale, reeked of tobacco fumes and frying, until Percy opened the door.

The cold was delicious. Clean and sharp, it took away Mikklau's breath, and the vast wintry silence restored the thrill inside him. Everywhere was white, the flat unfenced landscape stretching as far as he could see, untrodden snow from horizon to horizon. There was no sign of any other human habitation, no sound but his own and Percy's breathing. Apart from the tyre tracks on the roadway and a single set of footprints heading away across the parking lot, he and Percy might have been the only two people left alive.

"Where's Sam?" asked Mikklau.

"Gone, by the look of it," said Percy.

"Gone where?" asked Mikklau in alarm.

"Your guess is as good as mine," said Percy.

"He wouldn't have left without telling me!" said Mikklau.

"You don't know Sam," said Percy.

As if nothing had happened, he flipped the sign on the door from closed to open, then went back inside, donned his white apron, emptied the dishwasher and switched on the fryers. Mikklau followed, watched in bewilderment, not knowing what to do or what to say.

"You'd better dump your sleeping bag on the sofa for now," said Percy. "And we'll need logs for the stove. You'll find the log store in the back yard. I'll rake out the ashes and get us some breakfast."

"Yes," said Mikklau.

"Get a move on," chivvied Percy. "The first customers will be arriving soon."

Mikklau did as Percy asked, although his first impulse was to go after Sam, trail his footprints along the highway. But Sam could have hitched a lift to Halifax City, or else gone back to Jasper's Creek and by now be on a freight train heading south. The grief and shock of being without him changed into fear. In the icy back yard, where the pine trees brooded around a clapboard bungalow half buried by thorn-briars and crowlings fed in the garbage bins, Mikklau wondered what would become of him. And each time he passed through the sitting-room with his arms full of logs, an empty whiskey bottle on the coffee table, a crumpled blanket on the sofa and a lingering odour reminded him. He had been abandoned, dumped in a diner in the middle of nowhere with a man he barely knew.

Percy seemed kindly enough. He joined Mikklau at a table by the window, served scrambled eggs and waffles, toast and coffee. But there was a lump in Mikklau's throat when he tried to eat and he wanted to cry. Writing on the menu card, that he was unable to read, kept blurring when he stared at it and outside the sunlight turned watery. Then a lorry pulled into the parking lot with a hiss of air brakes and Percy rose to clear the table.

"Eat up," he urged.

"I'm not very hungry," mumbled Mikklau.

"Better bin it then," said Percy. "And mind you put the lid on properly. There's blooming crowlings breeding all over the place. You can have a burger or something later."

Mikklau stared at him – J. Samuel Hoddle's brother-in-law, an alien man with an immense paunch and countless chins who owed him nothing. But the grey eyes twinkled and a secretive smile played over Percy's ruddy features, as if he knew something Mikklau did not.

"Come on," he urged. "We haven't got all day. There's tables to wipe, bread to butter, vinegar bottles to fill. Let's be having you."

"Me?" said Mikklau.

"I thought you wanted a job," said Percy.

"I do," said Mikklau.

"We can talk about wages and rent for the bungalow later," said Percy. "Providing you like it here and we get on, that is."

"Bungalow?" said Mikklau.

"Well, you'll have to live somewhere," said Percy. "And *I* don't want it. What are you gaping at, lad?"

"Nothing," said Mikklau.

And even if he had wanted to, he could not have explained. It was something inside him, something that rose from the depths of his being, a huge upsurge of joy or laughter or triumph, he was not sure which. Grinning absurdly at the man who would employ him, Mikklau rose to his feet to begin the rest of his life.

The snow melted. Days grew longer and winter gave way to spring. Bearsbane flowered in the ditches in great purple masses. Mikklau did the chores, scrubbed the grease from the walls and floors, waited at tables and learned to use the fryers. He was a godsend, he heard Percy say. No local lad of his age would have worked so hard for so little money, and he had rid the place of crowlings, too. He knew a trick or two, Percy said proudly. He uprooted some bearsbane, planted it in pots by the septic tank and, every morning as his own people had done on the Reservation, he buried the food waste in the ground.

"Best day's work I ever did," said Percy, "taking him on."

Working long hours in a diner for low wages was not exactly what Mikklau had imagined for himself, but it was better than Gully Town, and use of the bungalow was compensation enough. Things that reminded Percy too much of Lou became his own. He cleared the thorn-briars from the garden, planted beans and carrots and potatoes. He knew how to live, boasted Percy, knew how to care for the land in a way their race had forgotten.

But something Mikklau was not much good at was taking care of himself. At first it seemed not to matter. Apart from Percy and the truck drivers there was no one to see the tears in his jeans, the holes in his socks and sneakers and the ripped zip on his anorak. He found needles and thread in Lou's work-basket but his attempts at mending were useless, and however often he attended to his laundry he failed to remove the stains or the creases. And the bungalow he had first thought of as home became more and more neglected. It smelled as Sam had smelled of unwashed bedclothes, grimy curtains and soiled carpets. It was lonely, too, and all Mikklau ever did was sleep there.

The prairie grass grew tall, rippled in the wind to the far horizon. The bearsbane died, and in its place water-bells bloomed yellow in the dykes beside the north-south highway. Gnats, with sunlight on their wings, danced beneath the pine trees on warm spring evenings. Carrots swelled among a fresh crop of weeds in the bungalow garden. They were ready for pulling, said Percy. But Mikklau did not know how to cook them and could not be bothered to learn. On a diet of fries and burgers served in the diner, eggs cooked sunnyside-up and apple-pie and cream, he was beginning to grow fat.

Two pairs of trousers from Percy's younger days, with six inches trimmed from each leg and enough room around the waist to allow for a further expansion in girth, averted the need to buy jeans. But, nevertheless, he was forced to take a trip to Jasper's Creek and spend the wages he had saved on larger-sized sweatshirts, another anorak and new socks and sneakers. The cost dismayed him. The pick-up truck he wanted to buy receded into the distant future many years ahead.

"You can't have it all," said Percy.

"Some people do," muttered Mikklau.

"And the rest of us learn to be satisfied with what we've got," said Percy. "Or not, as the case may be. But if you're not happy here, lad..."

It was not that Mikklau was unhappy, exactly. He had realised a while ago that within the alien society he would never amount to very much. For him this was all there was and all there would ever be: rented accommodation and working in Percy's diner. He could accept that now. He could accept that he would never live in Blue Water, gain a job as a managing director or go skiing each winter in the Lake Arrow holiday resort. It was not the lack of prospects, or the shortage of money, or the dearth of material possessions that created a yearning inside him. It was something far more important and far more precious than that.

As the weeks passed Mikklau grew more and more aware of it ... an emptiness inside him, a homesick longing, a need he could not define. He dreamed of the desert and the people he had left behind – Grandfather Ben and Grandmother Cloud, Skooa his father, old Kate Baxter, Ella and James. Percy was his friend, just as Sam had been, and most of the truck drivers he knew by name, but it was not enough. He wanted closeness, kinship, someone to make his life worthwhile and provide a reason for living. His days grew meaningless and all he did, apart from work, was exist.

Then, one morning when the sunlight gilded the miles of grass and the song-linni nested, before Percy and Mikklau had even breakfasted, a battered red pick-up pulled into the parking lot. It was piled high with things, furs and pots and a decorated native tent, and was driven by an elderly woman with greying red hair. Antique traders, said Percy, and too blooming early. But reluctant to turn away a customer he switched on the fryers and Mikklau unbolted the door.

It was then that he recognised them. Crossing the tarmac towards him were Kate Baxter, leaning on her walking stick, James beside her and someone else, a young native girl tagging behind them clutching Grandmother Cloud's red velvet trinket box – Rhawna, who Mikklau should have married. Sadness, gladness, pride and shame, joy and anger, a multitude of conflicting emotions warred inside him as they approached.

He held open the door and did not know what to say. Rhawna hung back, too shy to look at him or make her presence felt, but Kate's grey-green eyes, fond and familiar, gazed into his. Her lips brushed his cheek, and James grinned broadly.

"We're going to be neighbours," he said. "I shall be boarding at Halifax Academy just up the road, beginning tomorrow. We thought we'd drop in to check up on you, in case you wanted to come home." He stepped inside.

"So this is where you ended up," he remarked.

"Washing dishes," muttered Mikklau. "Like you said I would."

"Nothing wrong with that," Kate said stoutly. She hobbled past him and glanced round the diner. "You could have done worse for yourself and at least it's clean."

"How did you find me?" asked Mikklau.

"A gentleman by the name of J. Samuel Hoddle," said Kate. "He paid us a visit on his way down south. He thought we might be worried about you. Not that we had any cause to worry, of course. You're a man now, not a child. And you must be Percy," she said, limping towards the counter. "I'm Mrs Baxter. I've come on behalf of the clan to check on Mikklau's well-being."

"I treat him fair," Percy assured her.

"I can see that for myself," said Kate. "He's getting positively fat! We're very grateful you took him in."

"I wouldn't be without him now," said Percy.

"As long as you're both happy with the arrangement," said Kate. "And we may as well have breakfast while we're here. The young lady, by the way, is Mikklau's intended."

Percy stared at the girl lingering in the doorway and raised an eyebrow. Mikklau did not hear what he and Kate said next. Their voices were drowned by the whirr of the extraction fan and bacon sizzling on the griddle. Annoyed by Rhawna's presence and Grandmother Kate's remark, he turned to James.

"What did you bring *her* for?"

"She insisted," said James.

"She can't *stay* here!" said Mikklau.

"Surely, that's up to Percy?" said James.

"We don't make enough to employ someone else!"

"I don't think she expects to be paid."

"And we don't have the accommodation either!"

"Sam said you have a bungalow."

"She's not living with me!" Mikklau said hotly.

"She would have been your wife if you hadn't left."

"What's that got to do with it?"

"It's why she's here," said James. "And how she thinks of herself."

"Then more fool her!" snapped Mikklau.

"You never told her not to," said James.

"She had no right to assume ..."

"Then you'd better go and explain that to her, hadn't you?" said James. "Tell her she'll be going back to Tyler's Bluff with Gran and you don't want her."

Alarmed, Mikklau glanced towards her – a girl child, thin and shy as the forest deer in Grandfather Ben's stories. Knowing she was being talked about, her dusky cheeks flushed with rose and her feet, clad in beaded moccasins, shuffled awkwardly. She clutched the red box tightly to her breast.

He knew what it contained: all the dollars Grandmother Cloud had saved that he had once thought of stealing, now given freely, a marriage gift from the clan he came from, Rhawna's dowry that could become his if he accepted her. But it was not the money that swayed him. It was Rhawna herself as he approached her, a glimpse of something he thought he had lost, a feeling of reconnection.

The sunlight made a sheen on her long black hair, and her downcast eyes were purple as the belberries growing on the South Sierras. She would never be beautiful, yet she contained within her all the beauty he had ever known – the desert stars, the twin moons rising, the midday heat, the burnished sand. The wind that had touched her had once touched him, the sun and the shadows also. She had watched the crag-hawks wheeling, watched the sun rise over Tyler's Bluff. She had heard the clakka-snake and the river's song, felt the morning dew cold on her skin as he had done. Arms that had held her had once held him. She was the love of the whole clan come there to find him. She contained the past and the future within her. She would clean the bungalow, cook his carrots and mend his jeans. And when the nights were dark and he woke up lonely, she would be there for him.

She had goupa's teeth and knobbly knees but he would have to be stupid to reject her. And what he earned could keep them both. When, at last, Rhawna raised her eyes, Mikklau smiled.

"I'm glad you're here," he said.

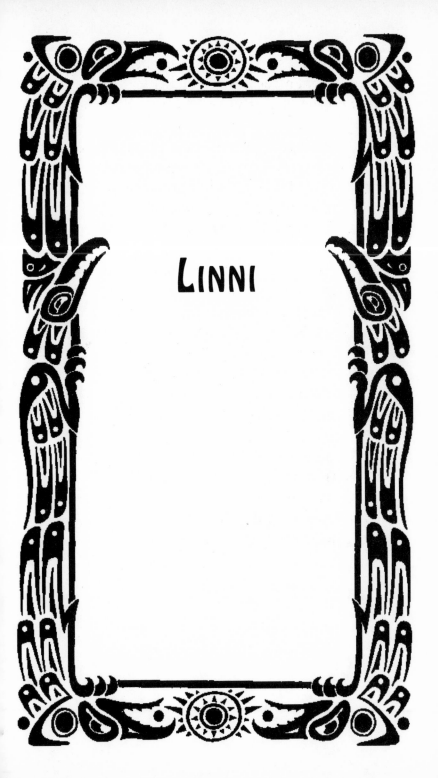

LINNI

inni dreamt that she was deep beneath the Northern Mountains. Somewhere an alarm buzzer sounded, but it was not she who woke. The dream still gripped her and in the cavernous darkness something stirred. A shape, not quite human, rose from its cryogenic berth, moved through corridors of dim light. She followed it, in her dream, to an underground laboratory, saw through its eyes and understood what it was seeing: a series of genetic eco-systems stored in glass-fronted cabinets – the desert, the prairie, the forests, the tundra. Here were the roots and seeds of plants, the frozen embryos of birds and animals, eggs of insects, spawn of fish, all that had ever lived on Linni's world stored in suspended animation.

Her dream continued. She seemed to share the creature's mind, share its emotions. An intelligence that was not hers checked the conditions. A hand, scaled and clawed, made microscopic adjustments. A sad heart loved and remembered. It remembered when ice-bears hunted and fire-eagles soared above the mountain heights. It remembered the great stone cities, their beginning and their end. Shaking its heavy head, it turned to examine the computer read-outs of the external biosphere, the minute fluctuations in the atmosphere of the planet. Linni heard the sharp intake of its breath, felt its dismay. Black wings, beating through the sky in its mind, beat also in her dream. Its clawed hand struck. Its strange echoing cry mixed with her soundless scream. And again the alarm buzzer sounded.

The alarm buzzer sounded and Linni opened her eyes, groped on the bedside table and pressed the switch. Cold daylight filtered through the curtains of her room. Arranged on the shelves, her collection of porcelain dolls gazed at her with blank eyes and, from the bottom of the stairs, Grandmother Rhawna shouted.

"Are you staying in bed all day, girl?"

Linni dressed reluctantly and went downstairs. It was a bitter Saturday morning towards the end of winter and, as usual, her parents were out working, leaving her alone with her grandmother.

The old woman eyed her tight blue jeans, her chenille sweater and her short-cropped hair disapprovingly. Linni had severed the traces with her native past. She travelled on a yellow school bus to Jasper's Creek High and no longer spoke her grandmother's language. Her friends, her lifestyle and her aspirations were all alien. Quite simply, Linni and Grandmother Rhawna had little to say to each other.

That morning Linni chose to ignore her grandmother, an old disgruntled presence warming her bones beside the oil-burning stove. Instead she sat on a stool at the counter, breakfasting on toast and coffee and flicking through the pages of a magazine, until the back door opened with a blast of cold.

Uninvited, Will Baxter entered the kitchen. "Hi, Linni. Hi, Mrs Crowling. Any news yet?" He pulled off his gloves and pushed back the hood of his parka, obviously intending to stay for a while.

"No," Linni said sourly. "And I prefer to be called Lynn."

In her chair by the stove Grandmother Rhawna smiled approvingly at Will. Links with his family went back to her childhood and beyond. The Baxters had always respected her for what she was and Will was no different. He respected Linni, too, if the girl did but know it. But her head was too stuffed with grandiose ideas about herself to accept Will as a friend. Sometimes Grandmother Rhawna grew tired of reminding her.

"You're native, Linni, and Lynn's an alien name that has no meaning. You were named for the little songbird that once sang in the forests—"

"*Once* being the operative word," Linni said crossly.

"No birds left now except crowlings," said Will.

Linni rounded on him. "What's that remark supposed to mean?"

"Nothing in particular," said Will.

"I know what you're getting at!"

"There's no need to get touchy, Linni."

"I'm Lynn! How many more times do I have to tell you? And just because my surname happens to be Crowling—"

Her grandmother interrupted. "Most of us are Crowlings now, girl, and no good denying it. The other wild creatures whose souls we used to share are gone—"

"And whose fault is that?" demanded Linni.

"Like our namesakes we have bred and destroyed—"

"Come off it, Grandma! It wasn't our fault that the crowlings mutated and got out of hand!"

"Here we go," sighed Will.

Again Linni rounded on him. "It's true!" she said. "It wasn't us who invented the organo-phosphates that altered their natures! And it wasn't us who sprayed the blasted things with pesticides until they became immune!"

"It wasn't me either," said Will.

"Your lot brought the technology—"

"And since when have you been willing to do without?"

"That's beside the point," said Linni.

"Is it?" insisted Will.

By the stove Grandmother Rhawna smiled again, a toothy grin of approbation for the boy who challenged Linni. Cold light shone on the counter tops as Will unzipped his parka and unwound the scarf from round his neck. He glanced at the cover of the magazine Linni had been reading. It was entitled 'Home Designer' and advertised an article within on luxury bedrooms.

"Thinking of going en suite?" he inquired. "Matching acrylic with a corner bath? Very nice, too.

Better than the dunk in the creek which you would have had a century or so ago, especially in this weather."

Linni switched on the expresso machine. Her bedroom was en suite anyway. And sometimes she hated Will Baxter, hated the ties of past generations that bound his family to hers. He was crushing and insufferable, just like his father.

The remark Mr Baxter had scrawled at the bottom of Linni's recent sociology essay still rankled. 'Economic Hardship' was a phenomenon she had never experienced. In the large house on Halifax Avenue she was separated from it. She saw it as the deserts of the unfortunate, the families who lived in the sprawling housing lots round the railroad station or the rural poor out on the western prairie, star-people and natives who, through their own failings, had never made good. May I suggest a career in eugenics, Mr Baxter had written.

"There's nothing wrong with being reasonably well off!" declared Linni. "Grandfather Mikklau worked like stink for the whole of his life to get where he did! And with three diners to run, my parents work like stink, too! Everything we have has been earned by hard work."

"Did I say otherwise?" asked Will.

Linni slammed the mug of coffee in front of him. "Just because your father's a school teacher and you can't afford what we can, doesn't give you the right to pour scorn—"

"Keep your hair on!" said Will.

The rocking chair creaked.

"We weren't meant to live like this anyway," said Grandmother Rhawna. "We should have stayed in the desert on the Reservation, or returned to the forests from where we came, stuck by the old ways. But your Grandfather Mikklau would never listen."

Linni stared at her. Grandmother Rhawna lived in a time warp, clung to her nativeness and refused to change. She dressed as she always had in a pair of shabby moccasins and a fringed leather skirt, decades old, that she refused to be without. Her face was lined and her hair was as white as the snow outside, a single long plait that hung heavily down her back. A tattered woven shawl was draped round her shoulders and her eyes, violet as Linni's own, inwardly brooded on seventy-five years of memories.

"The forests are owned by the lumber companies," Linni informed her. "And the Reservation at Tyler's Bluff has been taken over by the oil and mining industries. There're hardly any native people left there now, Grandma. And living here is better than living in a tent!"

The old woman shook her head. "It is going against ourselves," she insisted. "Once we had our own kind of wisdom, but where is it now? We have lost touch with the land that gave us life. Forgotten how to feed ourselves and clothe ourselves and how to survive. We have turned our backs on the Great Spirit and even our legends are mostly forgotten."

"It's always sad when one culture subsumes another," said Will.

"Sad for who?" asked Linni. "The Great Spirit wasn't any different from your alien God! It was just another male conspiracy to exclude women from positions of power. And what use are legends anyway?"

"Dad says they're often mixed up with history," said Will.

"And some things women do better than men and always have!" said Grandmother Rhawna.

"Like household chores?" Linni said scornfully.

"We are the home-makers, yes."

"Well, I've no intention of waiting hand, foot and finger—"

Will stepped casually between them and leant against the stove. "Some things deserve to be preserved," he said.

"Like the stuffed bakkau in Halifax museum?" said Linni.

"There aren't many people left of your grandmother's age who can recall the stories told round the camp-fire and remember what it used to be like—"

"Don't start her off!" hissed Linni.

But it was too late. Grandmother Rhawna cleared her throat. Her eyes grew misty and her old voice began to chant. "There was a tale old Ben Crowling, Mikklau's grandfather, told him of when we were Luppa and lived in the forests of the north. Then men made their own naming and Ben who was the first Crowling wished to be Karrakeel."

"Karra-what?" said Will.

"Karrakeel," repeated Grandmother Rhawna. "Winged fabulous creatures seen by no living eyes for many a lifetime. Their image has survived in our symbols, and their likeness is carved among the hieroglyphs of the ruined cities. It is said they sleep beneath the mountains, the North Sierras, and when the need is great they will awaken..."

Linni stopped listening. She had heard her grandmother's stories too many times before. And if the karrakeel had ever existed they were as extinct now as the bakkau hacked from the glaciers of those same North Sierras, a thing of the past. Memories of her dream stirred in the depths of her mind and, just for a moment, she wished the legend was true. There could be no greater need than there was now.

She stared through the window. Fresh snow covered the lawn, froze on the sheltering trees and the shrubbery, and the creek lay ice-bound all the way to the Long River. But the bearsbane was showing, clumps of dull purple flower heads waiting to unfurl, thrusting through the drifts along its banks. Soon, inevitably, the thaw would arrive.

Fear gripped her stomach. It was happening already further south and nearer the sea. In Ohio City the first crowlings were hatching and the annual death toll had begun: daily reports on the television news of a vagrant savaged in a doorway, a child attacked on her way to school, a whole family killed on an isolated farm. It was very low-key reporting but soon, in a few days or a few weeks from now, the killing and the terror would begin to happen in Jasper's Creek.

Crowlings did not discriminate. People or cattle or someone's pet dog was all meat to them. And they could attack as easily in Halifax Avenue as they could in the prairie farmsteads or in the housing lots round the town centre. In school Sophie Jones' desk had been empty since the summer and nothing remained in the sheds of the closed-down poultry farm but bones. Since the spraying programme had ended, more and more crowlings survived to breed each year and this year they could hatch in billions. This year it might be Linni's turn – the massed attack, the toothed bills tearing at her flesh.

She shuddered visibly.

And from far away she heard her grandmother's voice. "Had Mikklau's grandfather become Karrakeel he would have united all the native tribes, according to the legend. But to my mind he's done it anyway. If today's men had to run for their naming we would all be Crowlings now, for there are few other creatures left." The old woman cackled with laughter.

But Will was watching Linni. "What will you do if the Emigration Selection Committee turns down your application?" he asked.

"Don't!" she pleaded.

"It's on the cards," he reminded her.

Down south in the cities on the gulf, and in the Blue Water District near Kennedy City, anyone who was someone had already departed. Rats leaving the sinking ship, Mr Baxter remarked, star-people returning to the stars, quitting yet another world they had rendered uninhabitable. Soon, from Halifax to the north and New London directly to the south, the next fleet of ships would be taking off, another unadvertised exodus for those who could afford a berth.

"Our money's as good as anyone else's," Linni said confidently.

"Money's not the issue," Will reminded her.

"And Dad's a member of the Jasper's Creek Board of Commerce, which is bound to count for something."

"You're still native," Will said brutally.

She glanced at him, frank blue eyes holding her own purple gaze. He reminded her, just as Grandmother Rhawna was always reminding her, that she was native, engendered by native parents and bearing, as many natives did, the hated name of Crowling. She had been brought up to believe there was no difference between natives and aliens, that beneath the skin they were all the same, and at school Will's father never tired of teaching it. But so far no one of native origin had yet been granted a passage on any of the departing star ships.

Now, looking at Will, Linni was forced to recognise the truth. With her dark hair, dusky skin and violet eyes, she would fail to qualify. The rich star-people would leave ... all the financiers and businessmen, mine owners and factory owners, politicians and police chiefs, everyone else who governed and controlled. The ranchers would leave, their stock eaten by crowlings. But Linni would be going nowhere. On a terrifying world among the remains of a civilisation that had never been hers, she would be left behind with all the riff-raff of the alien race.

Further south the disintegration had begun already. There were murders and shootings and riots in all the great cities on the gulf. Refugees headed north. Kennedy City grew lawless with the influx. And sooner or later, according to Mr Baxter, the same disintegration would occur in Jasper's Creek. The day would dawn when people grew desperate and money had no meaning because there would be nothing left to buy ... no food, no clothes, no fuel, no help or hope. In a decade or so, humans could be as extinct as bakkau on this particular planet.

"They can't turn us down!" Linni said desperately.

"Dad says you ought to prepare yourself," said Will.

"If they do, we'll appeal!"

"You're native, Linni. You have no grounds."

"It's not fair!"

"It never was for most of us," said Will.

Again the blue alien eyes levelled with her own and she knew what he meant. Poverty was not necessarily due to individual failings. And on Mr Baxter's wages, with a family to keep and a mortgage to pay, Will would be staying no matter what. And then, star race or native, they would truly be the same.

"No!" Linni said bitterly. "It's not going to happen,

not to us. We'll be leaving here. I know we will."

"OK," said Will. He zipped his parka and re-wound the scarf round his neck. "What about you, Mrs Crowling?"

Grandmother Rhawna drew her shawl tightly round her skinny shoulders. Her chin lifted, obstinate and proud, and Linni guessed what was coming.

"Gamma Centauri Five is my world," she stated. "It's not for me to leave it or any of our kind. We must stay where we were born and learn to live with it again as we did before."

"Don't be stupid, Grandma!" said Linni. "You can't stay here on your own. You'll be coming with us."

"I wouldn't bank on it," Will said softly.

Linni opened the door for him to leave. A shaft of pale sunlight broke through the massed clouds. And did she imagine, in the veering wind, a trace of warmth?

Houses emptied on Halifax Avenue. Pupils who had been at school one day were absent the next. Of the eleven missing from Linni's grade none had said goodbye, not even her closest friends. It was the old pioneering spirit, the principal announced. After three centuries it had begun to re-emerge, a wanderlust that caused whole families to uproot themselves, urged them on to discover new worlds among the stars. He lied, thought Linni. It was fear that drove them. And by the next morning the principal, too, had departed.

Another day passed and Linni grew more and

more depressed. The emigration permit her father had been expecting failed to arrive. Lessons seemed pointless, as dreary as the sleety rain which buffeted the classroom window panes and melted the snow on the sidewalks. Bearsbane flowered in the school grounds, gigantic crocus cups brimming with black treacly liquid. It smelt of crowlings, which was why the birds avoided it, Linni supposed. But this year its sickly rotten scent, stronger than the diesel fumes of the waiting buses, served no purpose. The crowlings were late hatching.

Salt slush grimed Linni's boots as she clambered aboard. Too many empty seats reminded her of her plight and she did not need Will Baxter to remind her as well. He came down the gangway towards her, a pleased expression on his face. Gloating, thought Linni, because he had been proved right. She brooded through the window as the bus pulled off, and the seat springs shifted as Will sat beside her.

"Hi, Linni."

"Why haven't you gone home in the car with your father?" she muttered.

"There's a staff meeting," said Will. "And are you still waiting to hear?"

"You know damned well!" she snapped.

He could have retaliated, reminded her that he had told her so. Instead, his friendly reasoning hammered the last hope from her. "In that case you can forget about leaving from Halifax," he informed her. "If the weather clears, the ships there are taking off tomorrow night."

"There's still New London!" said Linni.

"Will you never give up?" asked Will.

"It's the rest of my life!" Linni said hotly.

"Mine too," said Will. "And if you'd just face reality maybe we could talk about it. Predictions can be wrong, you know, and things mightn't be as bad as we think. As far as most people are concerned it'll just be the start of one more crowling season. And if the authorities maintain the food and gasoline rationing, clamp down on the media and keep the television soap operas running ..."

"Is that significant?"

"It could give us a head start at least."

"What do you mean?"

"We can leave before the mass panic sets in," said Will. "Go somewhere out in the wilds and start again."

"Who's 'we'?" asked Linni.

"Us," said Will. "Your family and mine. Think about it, Linni. Your people survived from the land for centuries before we came, so it has to be possible."

Linni frowned through the window. This was the world that she had been born to and Will wanted her to abandon.

"Are you saying we should revert to being hunter-gatherers?"

"No," said Will. "But maybe we could take over an abandoned ranch. There're plenty of them."

"And wait for the crowlings to find us?" asked Linni.

"Surely it depends how we live?" said Will. "I

178

never heard your grandmother tell of any trouble with crowlings."

"That was *then*!" Linni said scathingly.

Will rose to leave as the bus pulled in at the centre of Lincoln Fields housing lot. "Think about it anyway," he said.

Briefly, as the bus drove on towards the out-of-town shopping precinct, Linni did as he bade. But no one in their right mind would willingly swap a civilised way of life for a primitive one, she decided. For dollars and ration tokens she bought milk and bread at the supermarket and tried to imagine the work involved in producing it, the sheer drudgery of a self-sufficient lifestyle with no time left at all for enjoyment.

Yet Grandmother Rhawna spoke of it fondly, the village of small adobe houses where she was born and her childhood in the desert, tending goats and grinding maize for porridge. There had been time then to fish in the river, time to swim and play and dance in the sunlight, to sit round the fire and tell stories. Chores were shared, the old woman said, and working all day with her friends in the bean fields had hardly seemed like work at all.

Her grandmother's reminiscences flickered brightly through Linni's mind as, alone and lonely, she walked along Halifax Avenue. Maybe Will's idea was not so stupid after all, she mused. It must be nice to be part of a clan, to be close to people as Will was with his family. It was something Linni had never known. Apart from her parents and Grandmother

Rhawna, she had no other close relations ... and no friends either, now. On either side of the road the abandoned houses mocked her as she passed and her loneliness grew.

The afternoon had darkened and a stench of bearsbane drifted across the gardens. Or was it crowlings she could smell? Panicked by her thoughts, Linni began to run. Cold raindrops showered her from the overhanging trees. Her heart hammered. No cars or people disturbed the silence. And her own house might have been deserted, too. The garage was shut. No wheel tracks showed on the wet asphalt drive. No welcoming lights shone between the half-drawn curtains. But the back door opened to her touch.

"Grandma!" shouted Linni.

"I'm not deaf!" the old woman replied.

She was just a shape in the shadows of the kitchen, an obstinate old woman refusing to participate in the trappings of a culture that had never been hers. Linni switched on the light.

"Where's Mum and Dad?"

"Gone to New London to lodge an appeal."

"Since when?" asked Linni.

"Since they returned here at lunch time to pick up the post and found that your application for an emigration visa had been refused."

Linni's parents should have been home late that evening but when Linni went to bed they had still not come back. Nor were they there in the morning when she came downstairs for breakfast. The storms were bad over New London according to the radio, Grandmother Rhawna informed her, wind gusting from the south and torrential rain. No one with any sense would drive several hundred miles through that kind of weather if they did not have to. They had probably stayed overnight in a motel.

"So why didn't they phone?" asked Linni.

"The lines are down," said her grandmother.

"Have you tried Dad's mobile?"

"He left it on the dining table," said Grandmother Rhawna.

What should have been an ordinary Saturday became fraught with worry. All day squally rain lashed the glass as she watched from the front room windows. Cars in their hundreds drove along Halifax Avenue, but none turned into the drive.

"Something's happened to them!" Linni said frantically.

"If it has, there's nowt we can do," her grandmother replied.

Early in the evening the weather cleared. A watery sun showed between scudding clouds. But the television newsreel showed the main roads flooded between New London and Jasper's Creek, vast lakes of water where the open flats had been. Grandmother Rhawna was right. There was nothing Linni or anyone else could do but wait.

Later, alone in her bedroom, Linni kept vigil on the window seat. The sky to the north cleared completely and she saw the ships from Halifax take off, a dozen or more lifting slowly above the horizon, curving streaks of fire in the gathering darkness. They carried a cargo of lives towards the safety of the stars, but hers was not among them. Inwardly she began to acknowledge what Will Baxter and his father had always told her. She would be staying behind on Gamma Centauri Five. She would be staying to endure the loss of everything she cared about, the life she had now and the future she had planned.

Bright constellations blurred with her tears, until she thrust away her despair. There was still a chance. The ships in New London were delayed waiting for a window in the weather and the emigration authorities there would hardly ignore a personal appeal by her parents, even though they *were* native. She had to trust, had to believe. Finally, in a few more days, she would be on her way.

Worn out by her emotions, Linni closed her eyes, and briefly she slept. Again in her dreams she wandered through corridors of dim light, up stairways narrow and winding where a strange green phosphorescence glowed on the walls to either side. Machinery hummed in the depths of the earth beneath her, and a clawed hand punched the combinations of an automatic lock.

Stone doors swung open to reveal a snow-bound gully and the mountain slopes beyond. A creature, more alien than Linni could ever have imagined, emerged from the underground complex and surveyed its surroundings. Huge almond-shaped eyes beheld the abandoned ski-runs, the swaying wires that carried the chair-lifts, and an arrow-shaped lake glimmering below. Buildings of a holiday resort nestled on the furthest shore, but no lights showed in the grand hotels or in the plush winter cabins scattered among the surrounding pine woods.

The creature's gaze moved upwards to the crags and glaciers, the great cleft peak directly above it and the freezing stars. It saw the fleet of ships curve overhead and leave the planet's orbit. It sensed Linni watching it and turned its head. Moonlight sheened the scales of its skin and its great eyes were fixed on her face. The pallid web of a wind spread as it crooked its arm. Its clawed hand beckoned and its voice, snake-like and sibilant, hissed in her head.

"Come," it said. "S-s-save yourself. Come to our s-s-sanctuary beneath S-s-skadhu. Bring all who will follow. You will be s-s-safe here. S-s-safe..."

Linni woke with a start. Beyond the window the night was unexpectedly bright. The two moons glittered on the dark water of the creek, and just for a moment, beyond the reflections of her own face, Linni thought she saw someone standing there, a winged reptilian shape born from the shadows and her own nightmare.

Hastily she drew back. She was seeing things, hearing things. When she looked again the garden was empty, the house quiet. And even through the double-glazing Linni could smell the faint rotten stink of bearsbane.

Or was it?

She glanced up. Something scratched on the ceiling joists above her head, a sound small as a timber beetle sharpening its claws. She heard tiny chirrupings ... kiku ... kiku ... and the soft fluttering of wings. Eight fifty-seven ... red digits glowed on her electric clock ... and in a sudden upsurge of terror Linni fled.

"Crowlings!" wailed Linni.

"Where?" asked Grandmother Rhawna.

"In the roof above my bedroom!"

"Are you sure, girl?"

"Kiku, Grandma! I heard them twittering!"

"That's crowlings, right enough," Grandmother Rhawna agreed.

"We've got to get out of here!" Linni said urgently.

"There might only be a handful," the old woman objected.

"And there might be hundreds!" said Linni. "They could crawl through the wall cavities! Enter the air-conditioning system! Or peck their way through the skirting! We've got to leave, Grandma! Now! While we still can!"

"What happens if your parents come back?"

"I'll leave them a note," said Linni.

"Where will we go?"

"Anywhere," said Linni. "The Highway Motel. You pack your things and I'll ring for a cab."

Grandmother Rhawna made no attempt to move, just remained where she was in her chair by the fire. Gas flames flickered blue and yellow in the draught from the partly open door. There was no other light in the room. It was her habit most evenings to sit in the dark and listen to the radio, or simply to sit and remember.

"Grandma?" said Linni.

"You go on," the old woman said. "I'll stay here."

"You can't do that!" cried Linni.

"I'm too old to be gadding about at this time of night."

That was the end of the matter as far as Grandmother Rhawna was concerned. She hunched over the fire, motionless and impassive, warming her bones. Age had shrunken her, wrinkled her skin and addled her mind. In Linni something snapped.

"Listen!" she said furiously. "Without Mum and Dad, I'm responsible for what happens to you! So you're coming with me, whether you like it or not! Do you hear me, Grandma!"

The old woman turned her head. She could be difficult and obstinate, but in the end she usually complied. Now, however, there was something about her, a determination in the lift of her chin, a glint in her eyes that was more than a match for anything her grand-daughter might say or do ... and an undertone of anger in her voice that Linni had never heard before.

"Don't tell me what I must do, girl! I've been told all my life and all my life I've obeyed. Your father! Your mother! Your grandfather! I may not have questioned *them* but I'm not taking orders from you!"

Linni stared at her in some surprise. "It's for your own good," she argued.

"You wouldn't know what's good if it upped and

hit you in the face!" Grandmother Rhawna retorted. "You want too much ever to know what's good or right! Want this! Want that! That kind of wanting has no morals, girl! It is without conscience or any other kind of self-control! It is a wanting of material things that can never be satisfied!"

"Try telling that to Mum and Dad—"

"I'm telling you instead!" Grandmother Rhawna said curtly. "Too meek I was at your age ever to speak my mind. To please my husband, please my son, I turned my back on the old ways and added to the damage being done. But now my time is over, near enough. When the Great Spirit calls I'll pay my dues for my participation. I'll answer to the soul of the Luppa whose forests we felled, and to the spirit of Brown Trout for the fouling of the water. And so will you, girl, not with your death but with your life."

"What do you mean?" Linni asked fearfully.

The old woman sighed. "We who are old will be leaving this world in a far worse state than when we entered it," she said. "We shall be spared from the consequences of our mistakes. It is you, the young, who will suffer in our stead and make reparation."

The fire hissed in the silence. A section of a native marriage tent that had once belonged to Mikklau's grandfather hung on the wall above it, fading symbols of bears and birds on tattered leather, genuine ethnic art that would have been worth a fortune in Kennedy City a few years before.

"Just get to the point," Linni said impatiently.

Grandmother Rhawna turned to look at her.

"You can foretell what will be as well as me, girl. The knowing is in your heart and in your blood. It is time you began to heed your native soul. In a land stripped clean of its giving, when all your wanting is replaced by need, it is all you will have to stave away the cold and feed your hunger, all you can depend upon to begin again when the star race and the crowlings have gone."

"You're gaga!" shouted Linni.

"Am I?" said her grandmother. "Ah well, so be it. Too gaga to come with you, that's for sure. But I'll not see you leave empty-handed."

She heaved to her feet and shuffled across the room, bent and reached beneath the bed to drag out the ancient red velvet box that had once belonged to Mikklau's grandmother. Linni knew what it contained. She had examined each faded photograph a hundred times or more: Ben Crowling in his battered felt hat, his fat wife Cloud, Kate and Joel Baxter, Mikklau as a youth and the skinny girl who had once been Grandmother Rhawna. She had read the registration certificates that proved they all existed. Now, blowing the dust from its velvet surface and caressing it fondly with a gnarled hand, the old woman held it towards her.

"This is for you," she said.

"What use is that?" asked Linni.

"More than you know!" the old woman retorted. "Take it and go!"

Linni shrugged, accepted the box and made to depart, then hesitated in the doorway and turned to look back. Light from the hall showed the old woman's face, thin-lipped and determined, still vital with life. The two of them had ceased to be fond of each other years before, but Linni could hardly leave her grandmother all on her own in a house infested by crowlings.

"I can't just leave you!" she said. "How will you manage if Mum and Dad don't come back? I can't just leave you and walk away, Grandma!"

"Yes you can!" Grandmother Rhawna said fiercely.

"If anything happens I'll never forgive myself!"

"Crowlings don't usually attack at night," the old woman informed her. "I shall survive until morning, never you fear. Now go, girl! And remember who you are!"

Gripping Linni's arm, she thrust her into the hall, then closed the door behind her with a quiet click. And now Linni was truly on her own. Dumping the useless red velvet box on the telephone table, she pulled her winter boots from the cupboard beneath the stairs and donned her quilted parka, then headed along the hall towards the front door.

Emotions tore at her, fear and guilt and grief. As she turned the Yale key she almost changed her mind: until she glanced behind her. High up the stairwell she saw wing-shadows dancing on the walls, birds small as moths fluttering round the landing light. Crowlings did not usually attack at night, her grandmother had said, but Linni was not about to wait and find out. Terrified, she bit back her cry, left the house and Grandmother Rhawna, and ran into the night.

The wind was almost balmy, the darkness full of whisperings and patterings and the sounds of runnelling water. Linni sweated as she ran, her boots making spray, her footsteps echoing loudly along the Avenue. Brighter than the streetlights, the moons overhead appeared and disappeared between scudding clouds, and garden trees made eerie flickerings of shadows.

Linni imagined crowlings everywhere. Millions hatched in her mind and roosted in the roof spaces of all the abandoned houses. She saw black wings beating at the windows trying to get out, more lurking in every patch of darkness. Last year's dead leaves lying on the sidewalk lifted in the wind and turned into crowlings. Others fluttered in the privet hedges or crawled from the roadside drains.

She had no idea where she was going; somewhere, anywhere where there were people, where the orange glow of the lights eclipsed the darkness and she was not alone. But the out-of-town shopping precinct was closed when she reached it, the parking lot empty except for a bus about to head back to the town centre via Lincoln Fields. Linni ran towards it. She would go to Will's house, she thought in relief. Mr and Mrs Baxter would let her stay and they would know what to do about Grandmother Rhawna, too.

Aboard the bus her fear subsided and it was not

far to travel. But, minutes later, deposited among a warren of residential roads lined with purpose-built homes that all looked the same, Linni realised her mistake. Although she had been to Will's house before in the family car, she could not remember the name of the road nor the number of the house. She asked at the take-away and in the late night laundrette. She asked a man out walking a dog. She knocked on a couple of doors chosen at random, but no one knew anyone named Baxter.

She began to feel stupid. She had over-reacted, she thought. Half a dozen crowlings flying round the landing light were hardly likely to hurt her, so maybe she ought to go home. Perhaps, by now, her parents might have returned and be worrying where she was. And the taverns were emptying. A group of drunken youths came lurching towards her, whistling and shouting.

"Hello, darling!"

"Fancy a good time, abo girl?"

A woman hollered from an upstairs window.

"Shut it, you lot!"

Their attention turned and Linni backed into a gateway, cowered behind someone's hedge as residents came from their houses and the youths hurled abuse. This was the social degeneration Mr Baxter had talked of. Faces grew ugly beneath the streetlights. A few stones were hurled and, in the house behind her, a curtain lifted.

Then it seemed to Linni that the night exploded. There was a rush of sound, a stench of rottenness, and all that was vile between people ended in a few seconds of horror. Crowlings came, hundreds upon hundreds disturbed from their roosts in the surrounding area. Youths shrieked. Men fought and fell. Others ran, their hands flailing wildly, beating away the birds that fluttered round their heads. A woman standing in a lighted doorway became suddenly featureless, her face and head smothered by a black mass of tiny feathered bodies. Her screams mingled with Linni's, a long demented wail of sheer terror.

Backing away, oblivious of the door opening behind her or the shaft of yellow light along the garden path, she clutched at the sheltering branches of an ornamental conifer and hid her face, clutched and hid as a pair of human arms tried to haul her out.

"Don't let them get me!" she shrieked.

"Come into the house," urged a man.

Covering her head with a coat, he hurried her inside. Sirens sounded on a police patrol car and ceased as the door slammed shut behind her. Sobbing and hysterical, not caring about what happened outside or who lived or died, Linni let herself be led through a crowded hall and into the kitchen. Familiar voices surrounded her ... Mr and Mrs Baxter, Will's younger brother and sister and Will himself.

"Is she hurt?" Mrs Baxter asked worriedly.

"Did the crowlings get her?" asked Mary.

"I expect they've pecked her eyes out," Ben said ghoulishly.

"Shut up, you two!" snapped Will.

"Go back to bed!" Mr Baxter said sternly. He guided Linni to a chair. "Sit yourself down," he told her.

"I'll put the kettle on," said Mrs Baxter.

Linni sat. She was shaking uncontrollably and still sobbing, but she had found who she was looking for. The bright inside light half-blinded her when Mr Baxter took away the coat.

"Linni?" he said in surprise.

"Linni!" said Will. "What are *you* doing here?"

"There were crowlings," sobbed Linni.

"You're safe from them now," Mr Baxter assured her.

"At home," sobbed Linni. "They were up in the roof space when I first heard them, but when I left they were flying round the landing light. I tried to persuade her but she wouldn't listen! She wouldn't leave! She said crowlings didn't attack at night, but she was wrong! And she's there all on her own!"

"Who?" asked Mr Baxter.

"Grandmother Rhawna," wept Linni.

"Where are your parents?"

"They've gone to New London. They went yesterday afternoon to apply for an emigration visa, but the roads are flooded and they haven't come back."

Mr Baxter glanced at his wife and his voice was grim. "You fetch the first aid box. I'll start the car."

"We're short on gas," she replied.

"There's enough in the tank to get there and back."

"I'll come with you," said Will.

"No," said his mother. "I'll go with your father. You stay here with Linni. We shan't be long."

"But Mum—"

"You heard!" Mr Baxter said brusquely.

They were two competent adults, a nurse and a school teacher, taking on Linni's responsibility and setting her free. Her part ended with their footsteps in the hall and the front door closing quietly behind them, and what happened to Grandmother Rhawna was nothing to do with her now. She heard the rev of the car engine outside on the drive and wiped her eyes on the sleeve of her parka.

Will placed a mug of sweet tea on the table.

"Where's Mum and Dad gone?" bawled Ben from upstairs.

"Out!" shouted Will.

"How long for?"

"Just go back to bed!" shouted Will.

"Suppose they get eaten by crowlings?" wailed Mary.

"They'll be safe in the car!" shouted Will.

The answer seemed to satisfy a child who was young enough to know no better, but Linni knew that no place was safe from crowlings. And if anything happened to Mr and Mrs Baxter it would be her fault. She bit her lip against a renewed welling of tears.

"What if Mary's right?" she asked fearfully.

"How do you mean?" asked Will.

"Suppose your parents don't come back?"

Will glanced at the clock on the wall. It was ten to

eleven and they had been gone for less than five minutes. "Would you like a biscuit?" he said.

"You don't need to be polite!" Linni said bitterly.

"So what do you want me to say?" Will demanded.

"You'll hate me," said Linni. "I know you will!"

"Does it matter if I do?" asked Will.

She wanted to tell him that he was the only friend she had left, but they sat in silence on their separate chairs. The clock ticked away another ten minutes of time.

"They ought to be there by now," said Will.

"You could telephone," suggested Linni.

The telephone was in the hall by the front door and Linni waited alone in the small, tatty kitchen. It must have been quite nice once, she thought, sixty years ago when the house was built. But now there was mildew on the wall by the fridge, drawers of the units hanging askew and a tile missing above the sink. The air was heavy with stale food smells where the extractor fan above the cooker had been sticky-taped over. One end had come loose, she noticed. It fluttered in the draught from outside, a sound soft and sinister as crowlings' wings. Alarmed, Linni joined Will at the telephone.

"No one's answering," he said.

A cold, sick feeling grew in Linni's stomach. But shut in her grandmother's sitting room it was not always easy to hear the telephone ringing, especially if the radio was on or if they were talking. They were probably busy packing a suitcase and trying to persuade her to leave, Linni reasoned. Unless they were already in the car and on their way back, maybe?

Will switched on the gas fire in the lounge and stationed himself at a gap in the curtains. He reminded Linni of herself, how she had been throughout the day. Half an hour passed and he telephoned again but there was still no answer. He called the hospital. They were in the midst of an emergency situation, he was told. The town centre was besieged by crowlings and more and more casualties were arriving every minute. Possibly Will's parents were among them although their names, as yet, were not on the admissions list.

It was the same when he telephoned the local police station. Every available officer and patrol car was out on call, engaged in evacuating the clubs and moviedromes, restaurants and diners. All Will could do was give them the address of the house in Halifax Avenue and continue to wait.

"I'm sorry," Linni said wretchedly.

"Nothing's happened yet," Will said firmly.

But it had, thought Linni, otherwise Mr and Mrs Baxter would have been back long ago. Will was fooling himself just as she had been doing all day, hoping her own parents would come home. She realised now that bad weather would not have stopped them, and floods and fallen telephone lines were just an excuse. Something had happened to her parents too and she, as well as Will, had to face the truth.

195

It was quiet now in the street outside. Moonlight and streetlights shone through the gap in the curtains where Will stood sentinel, a dark shape against the pale lace netting. Suddenly Linni recalled the other shape she thought she had seen, a creature from a dream, pale against the shadows of the garden trees. She recalled its voice in her head and what it had said. Whether it was real or imaginary made no difference. They had to leave Jasper's Creek, now, while they were able.

"What will we do if they don't come back?" she asked.

"You tell me," muttered Will.

"We could leave, like you suggested."

The shape of him shrugged. "I suppose we'll have to eventually."

"Eventually might be too late," said Linni. "We ought to go sooner than that. Tonight was bad enough. Those crowlings probably got blown here ahead of the storm front. But what will it be like when the main hatching starts? It won't be safe anywhere then and there's Ben and Mary to consider..."

Will turned to her and his voice was vicious. "Since when have you considered anyone other than yourself? Two days ago you didn't want to know! You were off on the star ships and to hell with the lot of us! So what's changed?"

"Everything!" said Linni. "Everything's changed, Will. And if we're going to leave in the morning we don't have time for arguing."

"In the morning? What are you talking about,

Linni? My parents are missing, for Christ's sake! Doesn't that mean anything to you?"

"Mine are missing too!" Linni reminded him.

"So how can you sit there, making plans? We can't go anywhere! Either of us! Not without knowing what's happened to them."

"We know already," Linni said.

"What do you mean?" he said harshly.

She stared at the time on the video machine. "It's half-past three," she said pointedly.

Will sat heavily on the edge of the sofa. His voice sounded broken. "Maybe they're only injured," he said. "Or maybe they've just been held up? Maybe the car's run out of gas?"

"Or maybe they're dead," said Linni.

"No!" said Will.

"Whatever's happened, they're not coming back," said Linni.

In the grey half-light of early morning Linni rose from the chair. Someone had to make a decision. Someone had to do something. But Will just sat there staring at the gas fire, inert and unresponsive, refusing to hear what she said. *Go!* Grandmother Rhawna had told her. *Go! And remember who you are. The knowing is in your heart and in your blood. It is all you will have, all you can depend upon.* The old voice urged her and the creature beckoned from her dream. *Come,* it said. *Come to our sanctuary beneath Skadhu and bring all who will follow.*

Rain lashed against the windows as Linni went to

the kitchen. It looked even dingier by daylight, the drainer littered with last night's dishes, mugs and milk and tea-bags littering the counter top, a tub of margarine and the remains of a sliced loaf on the table. And the loose end of sticky-tape over the extractor fan let in the chill and a smell of crowlings.

Linni froze. She could hear them fluttering, hear the tiny chirrupings ... kiku ... kiku. Their nearness terrified her. Her heart hammered and she wanted to run but her reasoning told her there could not be many and a peck or two was all she would get if they actually entered the kitchen.

She moved quietly, searched the cupboards: emptying them of anything that might be useful or edible. She carried it all through to the hall, then made piles of sandwiches. She closed the kitchen door firmly behind her when she'd finished and went upstairs.

The curtains were drawn in the room Will normally shared with Ben but she could make out the shapes of the bunk-beds and the tallboy. Quickly she searched through the drawers. Socks, underwear, spare jeans and sweatshirts were dumped on the landing outside the door. Ben slept on undisturbed, but Mary woke the moment Linni entered her room.

"What are *you* doing in my bedroom? Where's Mum and Dad?" Her girl's voice was shrill and demanding in the silent house. At ten or eleven years of age, Mary was old enough to know the truth, but it was not Linni's place to tell her. She had never had any dealings with younger children and, anyway, she did not know for sure.

"Just go back to sleep," she said.

She closed the door and went to search the airing cupboard on the landing but the gloomy daylight failed to penetrate and it was too dark to see what was in there. Behind her, Mary switched on the light.

"What are you looking for?" she asked suspiciously. "And why are Will and Ben's clothes on the floor?"

Without answering, Linni dragged out two crumpled sleeping bags. And Mary watched, a child in a nightdress with eyes as blue as Will's, seeing and knowing too much.

"We're leaving, aren't we?" she said.

"Yes," said Linni.

"Now, this morning?"

"Yes," said Linni.

"Where are we going?"

"To the mountains," said Linni.

"Is Will coming with us?"

"Of course he is," said Linni.

"But not Mum and Dad?"

Sorting through the towels and blankets in the airing cupboard, Linni tried to ignore her, tried not to answer. But Mary persisted.

"Are they dead?" she asked.

And she had to be told.

"Maybe," Linni admitted.

"But you don't know for sure?"

"No," said Linni. "We don't know for sure."

Mary nodded. There were no tears, no denial, no recriminations. She simply accepted in a way Will seemed incapable of doing.

"I'll do my own packing," she said. "And when I'm dressed I'll wake Ben. I won't tell him about Mum and Dad. He cried when our cat went missing and he mightn't understand. Will we be camping?"

"I expect so," said Linni.

Mary nodded again and returned to her bedroom. Grateful that the conversation was over, Linni gathered up the pile of clothes and sleeping bags and went downstairs. But Mary was not quite done with her yet. She hung over the banister.

"Can Elizabeth Aldridge come as well?" she asked.

"Who's Elizabeth Aldridge?" asked Linni.

"She's my best friend," said Mary. "She only lives down the road. Her dad's on Welfare and can't afford holidays so we usually take her with us."

"This isn't going to *be* a holiday," Linni protested.

"Oh, please," begged Mary.

Linni paused. The snake-voice whispered in her memory. Bring all who would follow, it had said. Setting aside her reluctance, Linni shrugged.

"I suppose so, if her mother will let her."

"*And* Christopher Wilcox?" asked Mary. "He's Ben's best friend and he doesn't have a dad at all."

"I suppose so," repeated Linni.

"Yippee!" sang Mary. "I'll go and tell him." She thumped back upstairs to his room. "Ben!" she shouted. "Get up, Ben! We're going camping and Elizabeth and Christopher can come too! We've got to

200

go and call for them, so hurry up! Linni's doing the packing. And put your mack on! It's raining!"

Linni sighed, started to divide the clothes and food into four green plastic garbage bags. It was not exactly how she had expected to leave Jasper's Creek. She had expected to go in her father's car to the nearest Space Port. Instead she would be setting out on foot in the pouring rain with four young children heading for a mountain that only God knew where ... and the creature from her dream.

She thought of it, a reptile thing, strange yet familiar although she could not think why. Somehow, across the unknown distance, it had become linked to her eyes and her mind. She could feel its gaze boring into her back, its ghost shape manifesting behind her, come to guide her on her journey. She turned, hopefully.

Will was standing in the sitting-room doorway.

"What the hell do you think you're doing?" he said.

Will was outraged. Hauling Linni into the front room, he slammed the door and leant against it. Not only had she had the audacity to rifle through someone else's home without permission, she had also involved Ben and Mary in what was tantamount to an act of madness.

"It might interest you to know that Ben and Mary are *my* brother and sister!" snapped Will. "You can't just take them away without so much as a by-your-leave!"

"I assumed you'd be coming with us," said Linni.

"You assume too much!" Will said angrily. "You've assumed your own mother and father are dead! And mine, too, when they mightn't be! We can't go anywhere until we know!"

"What difference will knowing make?"

"They're our parents, for Christ's sake! Yours and mine! And your grandmother as well! If they're dead, who's going to make the funeral arrangements?"

"The Welfare Services will see to—"

"How can you be so callous, Linni? And what if they're all still alive? They could be hurt! Hospitalised! In intensive care! We'll need to be here for them when they come home!"

"We need to ensure our own survival, Will."

"You always have been self-obsessed!"

"It's what they'd want us to do!" argued Linni. "Most parents put their children first! Even animals! It's a natural instinct!"

Will prowled the carpet. His initial anger had burnt itself out, but his face remained obstinate. If he refused to come with her she would leave anyway, Linni thought determinedly. And she would take Ben and Mary with her, no matter what he said. But finally Will nodded.

"OK," he said. "Maybe you're right and Mum and Dad would put us first; but is leaving Jasper's Creek the best option we have? What you're planning is nothing short of lunatic, Linni! It's all very well to say we'll head for the mountains, but how are you going to survive when you get there? You can't take kids of

Ben and Mary's age on a five-hundred-mile hike into nowhere! And it's pouring with rain, too. They'll be soaked to the skin before we even reach the North-South Highway!"

"They've got mackintoshes," said Linni.

"Better if we wait," Will insisted.

"Wait for what?" asked Linni.

"Just wait ... that's all. Wait and see what happens. Or at least wait until the weather changes. That makes sense if nothing else does, surely?"

Linni hesitated. For a moment she was tempted. If she were honest she did not really want to go anywhere, certainly not on her own with Ben and Mary. And perhaps it would do no harm to wait until the rain stopped? Or until they had found out for sure what had happened to their parents? A delay of a day or two would make no difference. She was about to agree when Mary opened the door.

"Me and Ben are ready," she announced.

"We're not going yet," said Will.

"When *are* we going?"

"When I say so," said Will.

"Linni said we were going this morning."

"Linni made a mistake," said Will.

But his words were a lie. The only mistake Linni had made was the mistake her whole race had made. As Grandmother Rhawna had done and thousands of native people before her, she had been about to relinquish her own inner knowing and accept Will's apparent logic in its place, trust him more than she trusted herself.

Her chin lifted.

"It wasn't a mistake," she said firmly. "Crowlings don't usually fly in the rain or the dark, Will. We need to be gone *before* the weather changes, be away from the town lights by nightfall. So we're leaving now."

Picking up her bundle of food and clothes, Linni let herself out into the morning rain. She did not hear what went on behind her but before she reached the front gate the children followed, humping their own garbage bags full of supplies. Will came too, a few moments later, struggling to put on his parka and lock the door, yelling at them all to come back.

Paying no heed, Linni headed along the road. It was a strange scene that greeted her. On either side, front doors opened. Mothers, and sometimes fathers, ushered their children out. Boys and girls of Mary's age, others of a similar age to Ben, toddlers being pushed in buggies by their older siblings, all dressed up against the weather and carrying their bundles, spilled onto the sidewalk. Voices besieged her.

"You're Linni, aren't you?"

"We heard you were leaving."

"Mrs Aldridge told me."

"Can Alison come with you?"

"Will you take my Billy?"

"Will you look after Jane?"

"It's not safe here any more."

"It's all right for us to stay on."

"But not the children."

"You understand, don't you?"

"I'd take them away somewhere myself..."

"But I've got a job to go to..."

"An elderly mother..."

"And I wouldn't know how to manage."

"I wouldn't know how to survive."

"But you're native."

"It's in you, isn't it?"

"This was your world once."

"You know how to live in it..."

Linni wanted to run. She wanted the ground to open and swallow her. She wanted to scream at them that she did not know anything. So many children, so many lives dependent upon her was more than she could bear. But the voices insisted, begged and implored her.

"Take them, please!"

"They might stand a chance with you."

"Go with her, Deborah."

"Go with her, Andy."

"Do as she says and she'll look after you."

"What's going on?" asked Will.

They turned to him then, people he knew as Linni did not: friends and neighbours.

"You're doing the right thing, Will."

"Everyone's leaving who can do."

"Half the town is on the move."

"And we know about your parents."

"We'll look out for them."

"We'll tell them you've gone..."

Their voices faded as Linni walked on. And the children followed her, thirty or maybe forty of them, sad, silent and probably afraid. She could not afford to think how they felt. She could not afford to care. They were simply footsteps pattering along the sidewalk behind, a squeak of buggy wheels, a sniffle of tears, a nightmare happening for which she was responsible. It was too late now to wish she had never set out and it was too late to wish she had heeded Will, remained at his place and waited.

"Slow down!" he shouted.

But her only desire was to escape – from crowlings and children, Will and herself and Jasper's Creek. She quickened her pace and passed the gas station. Cars queued for refuelling and Halifax Avenue, when she reached it, was jammed with traffic.

Families in cars and station wagons, in trucks laden with luggage and four-wheel drives, were all heading for the highway in a mass exodus from town. Speed was reduced to a crawl. Through partly opened windows Linni heard snippets from the local radio station warning of a break in the weather and a migration of crowlings to the area, advising people to stay in their homes and not to panic. But panic was everywhere. Linni could feel, hear it in the voices of passengers in every vehicle she passed, in the shouting and gesturing of stationary drivers and the frantic hooting of horns.

She paused in a gateway, and glanced behind. Muffled against the rain, with Will at their head, the group of children plodded along the sidewalk towards her. There was no panic in them. Whatever they felt, all their fear and bewilderment, was allayed by their trust ... trust in her and where she would lead them. They were hers now, every last one of them, belonging in a way Linni had never dreamed and did not know how to accept.

Yet she was bound to accept. They were her tribe, her clan setting history in reverse. As the children of the Luppa had been led from the wilderness over a century ago, so she would lead these children back. Among the noise and chaos of the traffic she waited for them to approach.

"Do you want me to go in?" Will asked her.

"In where?" asked Linni.

He nodded to the house behind her – her house and she had not even noticed! The front door stood open and there were no lights in the windows, no car on the drive, not even Mr Baxter's. It meant nothing any more, nor anything it contained, but it might hold something for Will ... some kind of clue as to what had happened to his parents, some kind of hope.

"You may as well," she said.

"Is there anything you want?" he asked her.

"Just some spare clothes," she said.

He was not gone long. The house had been ransacked, everything taken that was of any value and the rest of its contents smashed. Mindless vandalism, Will said angrily. And there was nothing to suggest his parents had ever been there ... just Grandmother Rhawna's walking stick lying broken on the hall floor among a few black feathers.

"And this," said Will.

Into Linni's arms he placed the red velvet box, her grandmother's gift rejected as useless and left behind by both herself and the thieves. Now, it seemed, it was inescapably hers.

"What's in it?" asked Mary.

The children crowded round as Linni lifted the lid. The familiar faded photographs smiled up at her: the first Crowling in his battered felt hat and fat Cloud standing beside him, both no older than she and Will. They had led the children of the Luppa from the forest to the desert, a journey much longer than hers. Strange and strong was the kinship Linni suddenly felt with them, as if their spirits hovered round her, approving and encouraging, knowing what she did.

But they were not all that the box contained. Grandmother Rhawna had added a gift of her own. Among the official documents of births and deaths and marriages were snippets cut from newspapers and old magazines, anything to do with the traditional native way of life ... wild plants and their uses, how to build a kiln, a fishing creel, construct a drag-sledge or carve a canoe. Coloured reproductions of ethnic art caught Linni's attention, symbolic representations of birds and fish and animals ... the bakkau, the ice-bear, the mythical karrakeel.

She stared transfixed. It was the creature from her dream, its reptile shape, its webbed wings, its huge almond-shaped eyes. It was neither a myth nor a symptom of her own madness and it never had been. It was real. And somehow its mind had become linked to hers, knowing her need. She had seen the mountains through its eyes, a great cleft peak, an open doorway leading into its underground sanctuary. It had called her to come there with all who would follow. Her eyes shone as she closed the box.

"What was that thing?" asked Will.

"A dragon," said Mary.

And louder than the honking traffic, Linni laughed.

At the junction to the highway the traffic from Jasper's Creek joined with other traffic from the south, everything turning north and heading towards Halifax to cross the Long River. In campsites in the forests or in the towns on the tundra, in an area where spring came late, summers were short and crowlings were few, they hoped to find sanctuary. For several miles in a choking wake of blue exhaust fumes and watery swirls of gasoline colours, Linni followed the same route and Will and the children followed her, walking in single file along the roadside pushing buggies or carrying their bundles, rain beating against their backs and dripping from the hoods of their parkas.

There was nowhere to shelter. Mikklau's Diner, almost ten miles from town, where Linni had hoped to wheedle a meal for them all, was crowded to capacity. Heads down, shoulders hunched against the rain, they were obliged to pass it by and eat as they travelled, a few sodden sandwiches from their supplies.

All afternoon they walked, the triple lines of traffic

still shuddering past them. And darkness fell early that evening, the rain turning to drizzle, wheels spraying their legs with water. They were all wet and cold and tired and hungry, said Will. They needed a place to stop and somewhere to spend the night.

"Where do you suggest?" asked Linni.

"You mean you don't know?" said Will.

"I can't think of everything!" Linni retorted.

"You're in charge of this stupid escapade!" said Will. "And sleep is as essential as food, for goodness' sake!"

"Take them all home if you don't like it!"

Annoyed, Will walked back along the line of children and returned a few minutes later. There was a farmstead a few miles along the next turn off, he informed her curtly. It was owned by David Anstey's uncle and, hopefully, they could stay there and use the facilities.

Normally Linni would never have dreamt of knocking on someone's door and asking for shelter, but nothing was normal any more. She was as wet and cold and tired as everyone else. Her hands, clutching her bundle and the red velvet box, were frozen numb. And any hope she had harboured that the karrakeel would come to her aid had dissipated several hours ago.

The darkness deepened when they left the highway. Only the moons, hidden by clouds, made an eerie shine on the road ahead and yellow lights of remote farmsteads glimmered like fallen stars in the black immensity of the land.

Linni was not sure how far they walked. It was automatic now to set one foot before the other, on and on through the drizzling night. She barely noticed the barns and outbuildings, bright security lights illuminating the yard, the front door opening and the exclamations of surprise and consternation. Who ushered her inside she did not remember. All she recalled was a bliss of warmth, a crowded kitchen and a meal of ham and eggs and French fries, a woman named Aunty Beatty, a man named Uncle George, a quiet front room and a sofa on which to sleep.

She awoke the next morning to sunlight streaming through a gap in the curtains, an ache in her leg muscles and the scent of freshly baked bread. Voices of children playing about the barns drifted through the partly open door. Who had roused them and dressed them, and where Will was, Linni did not want to know. She moved stiffly, pulled on her jeans and ran her fingers through her short-cropped hair to smooth out the tangles.

In the sun-filled kitchen Aunt Beatty gave her a buttered crust and a bowl of creamy porridge. She ate, gratefully, lingered over a mug of steaming coffee and listened to the radio. Pots of red geraniums bloomed on the windowsill and the door was open to the sounds from outside ... banging and hammering, cattle lowing in the covered yard, and children shrieking and laughing on the first warm day of spring. It was as if the world that had seemed changed for ever yesterday had reverted to normality again. But, among the musical requests on the radio, warnings of massed movements of crowlings were reiterated. And Aunt Beatty, packing ham and cheese and hunks of bread in a wicker basket, reminded Linni they would soon be moving on.

"That should keep you going for a while," the farm wife declared.

"It's very good of you," Linni murmured.

"They're children," Aunt Beatty said simply. She closed the lid and humped the basket to the doorstep. "Where will you take them?" she asked.

"To the mountains," said Linni.

"That's more than five hundred miles!" Aunt Beatty exclaimed. "I'd make for Halifax if I were you. Head for the forests on the other side of the Long River. Not much lives in those fir plantations and that includes crowlings. You might even find an empty holiday cabin..."

Linni stopped listening. It was advice that went against the karrakeel's instructions and she did not want to hear it. Outside the hammering had stopped and, from the dark interior of a ramshackle barn, a group of boys pushed a stout wooden hand-cart on its maiden voyage round the yard. Car tyres on a single axle jolted over stones and concrete and its small passengers bounced and shrieked in delight. Uncle George nodded his satisfaction.

"That'll do you, I reckon."

Will dragged a roll of heavy-duty polythene from the barn and heaved it on board. His face was streaked with sweat and dirt and, just for a moment, Linni warmed to his presence. He had taken care of one practicality at least. They would sleep dry in the open if they had to ... and warm, some of them. Aunt Beatty supplied blankets along with the food. The hamper was loaded. Linni's red velvet box with its precious symbol painting was stowed on board. Buggies were packed and, leaving Will to organise the children and say their goodbyes, Linni set out.

She turned west at the farm gate and headed on along the narrow lane in the opposite direction from Halifax. She heard someone shouting about going the wrong way but she paid no heed. Buggies and the cart, Will and the children, came hurrying after her and a runner sent to catch up with her repeated the same message.

"You're going the wrong way!" said the boy.

"No I'm not," said Linni.

"Uncle George says..."

Again Linni stopped listening. There was no point in arguing with a child. The boy went running back to Will to report her ignorance. He did not know she was not ungrateful. They had done what they could, Aunt Beatty and Uncle George. They were good people, kind people, and what was happening in the world was not their fault. They did not deserve what was coming: the destruction of their civilisation, as Mr Baxter described it. They did not deserve to have their property pillaged, perhaps, by refugees, or starve when the eco-system was destroyed, when the soil turned sterile and the food crops failed because all other birds, insects and animals had been devoured by crowlings. They did not deserve to be attacked and pecked to death...

A sudden shadow blotted out the sun and Linni turned swiftly, filled with dread. Will and the children too, were all looking back at the eastern skyline. Eyes widened. Faces paled. And Linni did not need to hear their frightened cries to know what she was seeing. Crowlings! In the distance the sky was black with them, a moving blackness of millions upon millions of wings, thick as cloud and curling like smoke. Even from where she stood, fifteen or more miles away, she could hear their noise and smell their stench borne on the wind towards her.

Back in the farmyard, maddened by terror, beef cattle bellowed and thrashed in their covered shed and Aunt Beatty called and beckoned from the farmstead doorway.

"Come back inside! Quickly! Quickly!"

"Linni!" shouted Will. "We're going back to the farm!"

But the karrakeel called, its snake-voice whispering in her mind. And her own instinct, the nativeness Grandmother Rhawna had urged her to trust, told her not to go back.

"No!" she cried. "We've got to go on!"

"We can't!" shouted Will. "We'll be caught in the open!"

"There's a copse up ahead!"

"It's miles away!"

"We'll make it if we run!"

Will had no choice, for Linni was running already, her feet pounding along the road. Moments later she heard the children following, the rattle of the cart, the squeak of buggy wheels, toddlers wailing and small girls crying. She slowed her pace until they caught up with her. And the shadow of the crowlings came nearer, their massed darkness slowly devouring the eastern sky.

The copse Linni was aiming for was further than she had thought and nowhere near the road. They had to abandon the cart and buggies, carry the toddlers and the basket of food across a ploughed field. Wet mud clagged their boots and shoes and the birds were almost upon them when they finally entered the wood. The leafless trees stirred in the rush of crowlings' wings and offered scant cover. But the sodden ground was overrun with bearsbane. Great purple crocus-cups, high as the youngest child and brimming with foul liquid, provided a kind of sanctuary.

They squatted among them, breathless and terrified, as the crowlings wheeled in the overhead sky. So many of them. Linni had never dreamed of so many. They seemed to be everywhere, whirling like black snow, a deadly blizzard of birds. The air was alive with them, thrumming with noise. Masses split into vast flocks and then reformed into masses, split and reformed and split again, veered away to the west and the north as those in the east swirled groundwards.

Linni watched them from between the trees, a

black tide settling on the distant margins of the land, on the roof of the farmstead and the roofs of the barns, beyond and beyond as far as she could see.

Gradually the sky cleared and the sun shone brightly again. Small sounds reasserted themselves: a songbird warbling, safe in its nest among the bearsbane; a child sobbing; Will moving beside her. She glanced at him and his face was as anguished as his voice.

"George and Beatty don't stand a chance!"

"No," murmured Linni.

"And did you see where the main bunch landed?"

"Jasper's Creek," she said.

"My parents..."

"Don't!" Linni said fiercely. "Don't think about it, Will!"

He was silent for a moment. His knuckles clutching the food basket were white and tense. His blue eyes brooded across the fields to where they might have been. "How did you know?" he said.

"Know what?" asked Linni.

"Just now," he said. "And yesterday. If we'd stayed in Jasper's Creek another day – if we'd gone back to the farmstead—"

"Don't!" she repeated.

"So how did you know?"

Linni chewed her lip, unsure of what to tell him. But somewhere in the mountains the karrakeel waited and, sooner or later, Will was going to learn of its existence. It was not a myth, she said. It must have evolved from a different species or else had come to the planet from the stars, as Will's race had done.

"I dreamt of it twice," she said. "Then I saw it beckoning from the garden and heard it speaking inside my head. I heard it again just now, telling me not to turn back. I think it's linked to me in some way. It sees through my eyes and knows where I am. It's watching out for us, Will."

Her voice faltered.

Will's face was grim. "That's what we tell them, is it?"

"Tell who?" asked Linni.

"The children," said Will. "Never mind about crowlings, there's some winged prehistoric reptile waiting for them up ahead? That should do wonders for their nightmares!"

Linni glanced round. Frightened eyes and tearstained faces watched her from among the bearsbane. "We don't need to tell them anything," she said.

"Typical!" said Will. "Children aren't stupid, Linni! And nor am I! We're all together in this, right? And we need to be kept informed as to what's going on!"

"I've just told you," said Linni.

"Listen!" Will said angrily. "If a creature like that had really existed on this planet we'd have known of it long ago."

"Not if it was in suspended animation."

"Oh, come off it, Linni!"

"It's what I saw, Will. A whole underground complex with scientific laboratories and cryogenic berths. They're obviously a highly technologically advanced race."

"That was a dream," Will reminded her.

"Suppose it wasn't?" she said.

"Try pulling the other one!"

"You didn't say that when Grandmother Rhawna—"

"That was different."

"Why was it different? History and legend are often mixed up together."

"For crying out loud!" said Will. "You can't seriously expect me to believe— It's a fairy tale, Linni! And whatever you dreamed and thought you heard wasn't real! You can't take us on a five-hundred-mile tramp up the flipping mountains on the strength of an hallucination! We can't survive up there!"

"My people did!" Linni said hotly.

"That was a hundred and fifty years ago and they knew how!"

"We can learn!"

"I can't see you surviving anywhere without a vanity basin and all mod cons!" snapped Will.

"So where do you suggest we go?" Linni asked angrily.

"North into the forests," said Will. "Like Uncle George and Aunt Beatty advised."

"And where do we cross the Long River?" asked Linni. "The nearest bridge is at Halifax and we can't go that way, can we? Those crowlings are between us and the main road."

"There are crowlings ahead of us whichever way we go."

"If we went far enough west," Linni said slyly, "we might find another crossing place. Or maybe an empty ranch house we could live in. That was your original idea, wasn't it?"

"At least it's a bit more practical than your hare-brained scheme," said Will.

"We'll have to travel at night," she reminded him.

"You mean we're stuck in this stinking copse for the rest of the day?"

"We're safe here, Will. The bearsbane will hide our scent."

"You'd better be right!" Will said fiercely.

He turned his back on her then and gathered the children round him. In a low voice he began to explain. They were going to wait for darkness and then head west. Eventually they might find an empty ranch house, he said, and learn to farm the land. They could keep bees and a milk cow, pigs for bacon and chickens for eggs. They could grow wheat and grind flour and make their own bread...

Linni stopped listening, squatted on her heels and leant against a tree. Will knew nothing about living from the land and even less about subsistence farming. And the vanity unit rankled. Remember who you are, Grandmother Rhawna had told her. But Will dismissed her along with the karrakeel, denied what she had barely begun to discover ... body, mind and soul, awake and dreaming, Linni was native and always had been.

They left at twilight and headed due west along the road. They were all tired, all tetchy, and between Will and Linni an unresolved conflict remained, differences that increased as the night grew later. Smaller children lagged behind. The boys pushing the handcart complained of blisters on their hands, others of sore heels and aches in their legs. And they were all hungry. They would just have to get used to it, Linni said brutally. But Will called a halt, held an impromptu meeting to explain why they were doing what they were doing and why they needed to go on. And five minutes later, back on the road, the whining and whingeing began again.

In the flat, featureless terrain there was no place to rest. Farmsteads were few, their welcoming lights switched off by midnight leaving the landscape dark in all directions. Only the road led on, shiny with moonlight, towards the far horizon.

Linni ignored the children's incessant complaints but Will gave in, stopped at the first shelter they came to, a Dutch barn in a field beside the road, its sides open to the night. On the dry ground within it, by a parked tractor, he spread the polythene and shared out the remaining sandwiches.

"You can't let yourself be ruled by them!" Linni told him.

"They're the ones who matter," said Will.

"They could have walked further than this!"

"What's the hurry?" asked Will.

"We need to get where we're going!" said Linni.

"Which is nowhere in particular," said Will.

"And now you've distributed all the sandwiches, how will we feed them in the morning?"

"We've got canned stuff," said Will.

"That's for emergencies!"

"Just get off my back!" said Will.

But for a while, at least, the children were happy. Little ones slept huddled together under a mound of blankets. Then, as temperatures dropped towards freezing, the complaints began again. Shivering in their coats and boots, the older boys and girls were too cold to sleep. Will was patient, solicitous, caring ... everything Linni was not. Her idea for warming them up was to get them back on the road for another ten mile hike.

"Push off!" Will told her.

She moved away, sat on her own in dampened straw at the barn's edge, her chin resting on her knees. She sat there for hours, alone, isolated, watching the two moons set and the slow shifting of the stars. And at dawn she watched the sunrise, welcomed its warmth from the depths of her being. It was the first time she had truly seen it, Gamma Centauri shedding its light on the land, and never before had she acknowledged her dependence upon it. She wanted to kick off her boots, take off her cumbersome clothes, dance for it, sing for it, as once her people had done. Instead she slept, comforted by its warmth, until a harsh voice woke her.

"Get out of here! The lot of you!"

There was no kindness in the farmer's eyes, no

giving. He was of the star race, believing he owned the land and everything in it. Useless to beg from him either food or water, although Will tried. Ushering the children before her, Linni departed. Hungry as they were, they would walk until nightfall, she decided. And across the fields, from the carcass of a once-live steer, a small flock of crowlings took to the wing.

Linni changed over the days that followed, warmed with the weather, softened like the countryside she walked through. Her senses were honed. As the vast prairie fields gave way to undulating hills of rough pasture where beef cattle grazed, or else lay as skin upon bones after the crowlings had feasted, she began to smell crowlings often from miles away. And her warnings had an uncanny accuracy that even Will was forced to respect.

And it was not only Linni who changed. The children changed, too, grew lean and strong from living out of doors and long days or nights of marching. They walked barefoot now, their blisters healing and hardening, their faces tanned by the wind and sun. They were hungry, always. Food raided from abandoned farms, or freely provided at the homesteads and ranches that remained occupied, was seldom enough. Hunger was something they learned to endure, a need that drove them westwards along the roads and farm tracks in the hope of finding another meal. In the deepening twilight they even made a game of it.

"I went shopping and I bought apples," Linni chanted.

"I bought apples and burgers!" sang a boy.

"I bought apples, burgers and chocolate!" shouted another.

"I bought sausages!" shrilled a small girl.

"Wrong!" came the chorus. "It's got to be something beginning with 'D'."

"Like dinner," said a boy.

"Or doughnuts," said Linni.

"You've changed," Will remarked. "You're actually beginning to communicate with them, at long last."

It was communicating with Will that bothered Linni. As long as they kept heading west towards the mountains, Linni did not feel compelled to confront him, but she knew she would have to sooner or later. She wondered what Cloud would have done if, long ago, Ben Crowling had refused to agree to leave the northern forests and make the long trek eastwards.

"I hate us living like hobos," sighed Will.

And there was the truth of it, the real difference between him and Linni. She could live without a vanity basin but he remained entrenched in the ways of the world they were leaving. He tried to cling to its civilised standards, imposed them on the children too, as if he feared them being so close to the primitive earth. He made them wash at every opportunity and comb their hair. And as they walked he taught them maths and history, chemistry and physics. He had them practise their reading on the signposts along the way.

The small unfrequented roads criss-crossed the land. Most were farm tracks ending in someone's yard, at another set of farm buildings that might contain cow-cake or mangels, or a ranch-house door that might open and admit them to a feast of French fries and eggs. A few led towards outback towns that Linni had never heard of ... south to Stonely and Crannock ... west to Smithfield and Bunyan's Bridge, the way they continued heading.

In the mornings their shadows strode before them and in the evenings they followed the setting sun. Finally, Linni saw what she had seen through the eyes of the karrakeel so long ago ... a chain of mountains on the far horizon, the snow-clad ridges of the North Sierras ... and one in particular, far to the north, its cleft peak rising stark against the sky.

She lost sight of it as they drew nearer. The landscape grew wilder and more rugged, just miles of rough grazing. The spaced-out farmsteads were locked and shuttered and there was nothing left alive upon the land, just evidence of goupa burrows among tussocks of grass, although goupas themselves were almost extinct, poisoned as agricultural pests decades ago.

The moment grew nearer when Will and Linni would clash. Several times Will was inclined to take possession of one of the abandoned farms but always Linni persuaded him to go further ... just another few miles, or another day or so of walking. Somewhere nearer a town where there might be supplies, perhaps? Then, where the scree slopes rose to the mountain heights, the westerly road ended in a two-way junction. North and south the signpost pointed. Thirty-nine miles north to Bunyan's Bridge and fifteen miles south to Smithfield, read the children. Their voices besieged her.

"Smithfield's nearer."

"We could be there by tonight."

"Let's go to Smithfield, Will!"

"It might have a supermarket."

"Or a burger bar."

"It might have a laundrette, too," said Will.

"It's the wrong direction," Linni objected.

"The wrong direction for where?" asked Will.

"We need to head north."

"Why north?"

"You wanted to go north in the first place, Will. You wanted to head for the forests, remember?"

"We need to find a ranch house, somewhere to settle."

"It's not safe on this side of the river."

"When's the last time we saw any crowlings?"

"We've seen where they've been," said Linni.

"Been and gone," said Will. "There's nothing left around here that's eatable so they've no reason to return, have they?"

"And I want to go to Smithfield!" Mary said fiercely.

"So do I!" came the chorus.

"It seems you've just been out-voted," said Will.

The boys turned the handcart with its cargo of blankets, discarded coats, cow-cake and mangles and foot-weary toddlers. The girls turned their buggies containing younger children, and the whole group set off south towards Smithfield. Linni remained where she was, her noon-day shadow small at her feet, her senses reaching out across the sunlit miles of grass and scrub. Dust devils danced in the distance and the land was dry and stony, semi-desert, useless for growing wheat or beans or any other subsistence crop. Young voices called to her.

"Come on, Linni!"

Defiant, Linni turned north towards Bunyan's Bridge and did not look back. It was a gamble that paid. They shouted and hollered but, eventually, they followed, the handcart and buggies being pushed at a run in an effort to catch up with her. She slowed her pace until they were close behind, their voices angry and muttering, then strode on. Furious, Will gripped her arm.

"You've no right to do this, Linni! It's emotional blackmail! Undemocratic! We voted to go to Smithfield!"

Linni shook herself free. "You weren't bound to follow me!"

"What else did you expect us to do?"

"This way is better anyway," she said.

And her reasons were sound enough. If they wanted to settle they would be wiser to choose somewhere near Bunyan's Bridge than out in the dry lands by Smithfield. There would be rich soil beside the river, a constant water supply and the forests beyond would supply fuel for the winter. There was sure to be a supermarket there, too, she told the children. They could go swimming in the river and they might even find a boat and some fishing gear.

"Fresh trout," said Linni. "Grilled over an open fire. Think of it! And it's only a few miles further."

"Actually, it's more than twice as far!" said Mary.

"Only another day's walking," said Linni.

"And I want to go fishing," said a boy.

"Very well!" Will said crossly. "We'll go to Bunyan's Bridge then. Satisfied, now?" he said to Linni.

All day they walked. And the road ran past a ruined city nestling at the foot of the mountains, its crumbling walls buried by thorn-briars. It had been constructed more than five thousand years ago, Will informed the children, from solid blocks of stone so huge and heavy that no modern-day machine could lift them, and so finely butted that not even a razor blade could fit between them. And from the air, fanning out from the city over many miles, lines of irrigation ditches could be seen, suggesting that this whole area had once been intensively farmed. There were other similar cities elsewhere, vast ruined metropolises surrounded by dried-up hinterlands. Archaeologists could only presume from the carved hieroglyphs that, once upon a time, the native people of Gamma Centauri Five had been a highly advanced civilisation.

He was wrong about that, thought Linni, although she could not think why. It was just a knowing locked away in her memory and refusing to come to the surface.

227

"What happened?" asked one of the boys.

"No one knows," said Will. "Wars? Famine? Disease? It happened on the planet we came from, too ... the rise and fall of civilisations."

And it was happening again, thought Linni, except that Will refused to accept it. What he was searching for was not a new beginning but somewhere to continue the civilisation he had always known for a few years more. In a fully equipped ranch-house near to Bunyan's Bridge and, hopefully, undiscovered by crowlings, he would seek to delay the end that was inevitable.

They spent the night and the following night sleeping on the dry grass by the roadside, rose at dawn and approached the town in the early morning. They could see it in the distance from a low hill top, a green oasis on either side of the river with trees and water meadows and white clapboard houses. There was a school and a church and a stone-built bridge arching above its own reflection, a wooded ridge beyond. It was everything Linni had said it would be and everything Will desired.

"You were right," he admitted.

"About what?" asked Linni.

"Bunyan's Bridge is a good place to stop."

It was good enough even for Linni, at least for a while. Excited children went charging down the hill towards it, buggy wheels rattling and the handcart swaying wildly, the riding toddlers shrieking with delight.

And Skadhu with its cleft peak was nearer now, its snowy heights dazzling white in the morning light, its ski-lifts hanging motionless above the dark serried ranks of pine. Linni guessed what it meant and, at the bottom of the hill where the green fields began, the children had stopped. Several horses lay dead in a meadow and, as the wind shifted, Linni smelt crowlings.

"I don't see any," said Will.

"They're here somewhere," said Linni.

They advanced cautiously.

"There's a person over there," whispered Mary.

She was a woman sitting in her chair on the front porch but when Will went to greet her he found she, too, was dead. Dead also were the children in the schoolyard, the preacher in the church doorway and the man in his car at the gas station. Spring flowers bloomed in neat front gardens, but nothing was left of the inhabitants of Bunyan's Bridge except bones among piles of clothes, and the bridge across the river was littered with blood-red dung.

Suddenly it became a grisly, ghastly place. No sound but the rattle of the handcart and the squeak of buggy wheels, the breeze through the rushes and the runnel of the river over its gravelly bed, a signboard creaking above the hardware store some distance ahead. Nothing alive anywhere apart from themselves, not even a fly. But somewhere crowlings were lurking, and somewhere an electric generator was running, and the lights were on in the supermarket, a dull glow against the sunlit street.

They stopped outside. It was a low prefabricated building selling liquor and ice-cream, its windows covered with advertising slogans for the bargains within. Children's voices babbled excitedly.

"We can buy sausages here!"

"And oven fries!"

"And burgers!"

"Who's got some money?"

"We don't need any money."

"Everyone's dead, remember?"

"We just go inside and take what we want."

"I want waffles and syrup."

"I want some chocolate chip cookies!"

In a space between the advertisements Linni pressed her nose against the glass. The inside was dark, despite the light, its electrical brightness absorbed by an overall blackness ... black over the display shelves and check-out counters and freezer units ... and the pale linoleum floor was splattered with crimson drops that glistened like blood.

"Let's go in," begged the children.

"Can we go inside, Will?"

"Can we?"

It was then Linni realised what she was seeing. The blackness was alive. Red claws perched and preened. Tiny wings fluttered. Birds, small as chafer-beetles, thousands upon thousands, jostled for position, the striplights glittering in their eyes.

"No!" screamed Linni. "Don't go in there!"

Her warning came too late. Will had already opened the door. Inside the supermarket the blackness exploded as the crowlings took flight. In a black gale of wings they poured through the door before Will could shut it. There were crowlings everywhere then, fluttering masses exiting through open doors and windows of surrounding shops and houses, others crawling from drains and basements too bloated even to fly.

Linni and the children were attacked from all directions. Boys howled and ran, birds pecking at their exposed flesh, at their ears and arms and ankles. Girls cried and clung together. Smaller children wailed in the buggies and trapped toddlers screamed in the handcart. Linni shrieked, slashed her way forwards through the black whirling air and covered them with a blanket. She covered the girls and the buggies, too. There were birds in her hair, vicious and biting, toothed bills tearing at her arms and legs. She hurled them away, crushed them with her hands, stamped on them with her bare feet, her blood mixing with theirs. She saw Will fall and tried to reach him but there were too many of them. They smothered her with their vile bodies, with their twittering noise and their stench, stifling her screams and the screams of the children and the roar and hiss of flame.

Runnels of blood trickled into Linni's eyes ... yet she saw. On vast wings the creatures circled in the overhead sky. Six of them, she counted, each armed with a pack-weapon angled earthwards. Thin gouts of flame swept along the street and the birds began to fall. Charred bodies dropped like black rain and the air was full of flying sparks and a stench of burning feathers. Gradually, round Linni and the handcart and the group of children, round Will lying on the sidewalk and the fleeing boys, spaces opened up. Brushing away the crowlings that clung to her, Linni gazed upwards and still the karrakeel circled overhead.

"Dragons!" Mary cried fearfully.

"Fire-breathing dragons!" another girl sobbed.

"They won't hurt us," said Linni.

Snake voices hissed among the shafts of fire.

"Get out of there! All of you!"

Linni did not need to repeat it. The girls heard for themselves and understood. Some took the younger ones on ahead. Others helped Linni clear Will's body of crowlings, dragged him to the handcart and hauled him aboard. They shoved it together, running as the boys were running, towards the wooded hills beyond the town. The axle wobbled. Squashed crowlings bloodied the tyres and the terrified toddlers cried and clung, their eyes fixed on the sky.

"Dwagons! Dwagons!" they wailed.

Linni did not have the breath to console them. Shoving the handcart, she ran for her life. Buildings behind her burst into flames. Thick smoke billowed round her and the fiery smuts that were once living crowlings continued to fall. She ran past the riverside meadows and on up the long hill out of Bunyan's Bridge towards the edges of the northern forest where the boys were hiding.

"This way!" yelled the boys.

"They mightn't see us among the trees!"

Girls and buggies turned from the road onto a track made by timber wagons, but the handcart tipped on a rut as Linni attempted to follow. Wailing toddlers and a half-conscious Will spilled onto grass and raw earth. And there, in the aftermath among the snivelling and crying, among the dabbing of wounds and the communal terror of dragons, from a mound of mangels and blankets, Linni unearthed the red velvet box.

Taking out the symbol picture, she smoothed its creases. It was not exactly realistic, but it captured the essence of the karrakeel, its reptilian form, its huge almond-shaped eyes, its great webbed wings. And as Grandmother Rhawna had done so many times in the past, she gathered the children round her and told them its story.

Later they stood together at the forest's edge watching, silently, as the karrakeel circled above the town. Bunyan's Bridge burned with the lush land around it, all who had lived and died there being consumed by fire. A great pall of smoke darkened the sky where the winged shapes wheeled and glided. But there was no fear now in the children's eyes. They watched them in wonderment, knowing what they were.

The story Linni had told differed from her grandmother's in some respects. For her the karrakeel were real, not a myth. From dreams or experience, forgotten details rose to the surface and things connected up in her mind. She had been there when the first karrakeel awoke, had seen through its eyes, shared its memories and its sadness and heard it strike the alarm to waken its fellows. She understood them in a way Grandmother Rhawna had not.

Maybe the karrakeel, too, had come from the stars, she had informed the children, or maybe they had simply evolved here alongside the native population, and progressed into an advanced civilisation while Linni's people remained primitive. It was the karrakeel who had built the ruined cities, metropolises as big as Kennedy or even bigger. For their intensive farming they had, most likely, invented organo-phosphates or something similar, and the same thing that was happening now had happened then. The crowlings had mutated.

"I suppose most of the karrakeel population must have died," said Linni. "Or else they built space ships and escaped to the stars as some of your people have done. But a few remained in the laboratory complex beneath the North Sierras. There they stored the genetic material of everything that existed, ready to re-stock the planet. They must have taken us in, too, given shelter to the native people, because our legends say that the karrakeel are the guardians of this world and that we, long ago, were born from the womb of those same mountains."

And so, Linni went on, the planet belonged to native clans, and the karrakeel slept in their cryogenic berths, believing it safe. Five thousand years passed until, three centuries ago, another technologically advanced race arrived from the stars. And again the crowlings mutated. So the karrakeel awoke, as the legend said they would, to save whoever they could and give them shelter.

The children had listened, questioned and simply accepted ... they would be living with aliens beneath a mountain until it was safe to come out again. Linni had felt their trust shift with the direction of their gaze. It was the karrakeel they looked to now to supply their needs, not her. Temporarily, her part was nearly over; there were just a few more miles to go, on past the blue arrow-shaped lake and up the ski-slopes to the doorway into the mountain.

But for now she watched until the burning was done and the winged shapes came gliding towards her. They made no attempt to land. They just swooped low above the tree tops. Soft voices called her to follow, called to them all, and their vast shadows merged with the shadows of forest canopy in a brief fly-past. Then they veered away northwards back to Skadhu.

"Wow!" said a boy.

"They're incredible!" said another.

"We've got to follow them!" said a third.

"How much further is it?" asked a girl.

"Up past Blue Arrow Lake," said another.

"They'll be there long before us," said a third.

"Not if we hurry," said a boy.

Boys righted the handcart. Girls ushered the young ones into the buggies. And what life would be like in the karrakeel's underground sanctuary Linni could not imagine, but the children had their own ideas.

"Will it be dark, do you think?"

"They'll have torches, I expect."

"I wonder what they'll give us to eat?"

"Some sort of manufactured protein stuff, probably."

"Oh, yuk!"

"Or they might cook us burgers and fries."

"You can't keep cows under a mountain, silly!"

"But you can grow mushrooms, can't you?"

"I don't like mushrooms."

"Then you'll have to have the manufactured protein, won't you?"

In pairs and trios and small groups, and still chattering animatedly, the children regained the road. Forty-one, Linni counted, streaming northwards between the towering pines. Only Mary lingered, a barefoot girl grown tall, gawky with wild matted hair, concerned for a brother other than Ben.

"What about Will?" she said.

Linni glanced towards him. He sat alone against a tree, hunched above his own hurts, blood drying on his shirt and in his hair. He had been angry when he knew what had saved him from the crowlings, angry and hating, not wanting to acknowledge that the karrakeel existed. Linni could understand why. He had been wrong about them and wrong about other things, too. And it was not just Bunyan's Bridge they destroyed but the whole of Will's world, all his hopes and dreams and everything he had ever believed turning to ash.

There was nothing Linni could say to him, nothing anyone could say, although Cloud and the first Crowling, heading in the other direction after the destruction of their village, must have felt the same. But theirs was a way of life dying that should have gone on for ever, the only way of life this planet could bear. Clutching the red velvet box, she squatted beside him.

"It's not worth grieving for, Will."

"What isn't?" he said harshly.

"Everything we've left and lost."

"How can you say that, Linni?"

"It gave us crowlings, Will."

"It gave us other things, too!"

"Like vanity basins?" said Linni.

"Not all of it was bad!"

"We just have to forget it," she told him.

"Which is easy for you!"

"It's no easier for me than it is for you, Will."

"You're native, Linni. You're still close to it. But I don't want to end up living like an aborigine, hunting with a bow and arrow and grubbing about in the dirt for something to eat!"

Linni felt the hurt, huge, searing, squashed by her own cold thought. Now she knew what his true feelings really were. But the long trek had taught her that it was no shame to be who she was. And it was no shame, either, to bear the name of Crowling. The birds, like the planet, had been poisoned and corrupted, changed from scavengers to killers. Yet, before their food supplies ran out and their massed numbers dwindled, they would have cleansed the world.

Then the planet would be hers again, hers to share with the children from Jasper's Creek and anyone else who made the same journey, for Linni could not believe that she alone had been called by the karrakeel. And no matter what Will said, or how much he raged against it, he would be part of it ... a world re-stocked and re-seeded, even with crowlings, from a bio-lab beneath a mountain, a world without cities and motorways and gas stations, with no soda-light glows at night to dim the moons and stars, no sprawling estates of identical houses, no debt, no money ... just the great freedom of the land that none of them had ever known.

She rose to her feet. "I'm going," she said coldly.

"Don't let me stop you!" he retorted.

"What will you do?"

"Go back to Jasper's Creek," he said.

She wanted to scream at him. She needed him. Ben and Mary needed him. They all needed him. They were star-race children and they needed Will to remind them of who they were, of the world they had come from and the civilisation they had once enjoyed. What he said was true. It was not all bad. And when they came out from beneath the mountain, two years or five years or ten years from now, they would need him to teach them how to live. Linni on her own was not enough, nor the precious snippets of information in the red velvet box. They needed Will, too, the standards he set them and the man in him that balanced the woman in her.

She bit her lip, wondering what Cloud would have done, a hundred and fifty years before. This had been her land once, hers and Ben Crowling's, but what would she have done had Ben refused to leave it? Would she, like Grandmother Rhawna, have meekly complied with his wishes? Or would she have raged, or cajoled, or pleaded? Linni had no way of telling. But Cloud's genes were in her and she shared her strength and her blood. And if she trusted herself and her own inner sensing, she knew that Will had no choice.

Five hundred miles?

Alone?

All the way back to Jasper's Creek?

Through crowling-infested countryside?

On a matter of principle?

No one could be that stupid.

And Will was not stupid at all.

"Please yourself!" she said.

She returned to the road where Mary was waiting.

"Isn't he coming?" Mary asked worriedly.

"He'll follow in his own sweet time," Linni said.